BC

PENGUIN BOOKS
THE GOLDEN WAIST-CHAIN

Born in 1956, Sara Rai grew up in Allahabad and New Delhi. After graduating from Lady Shri Ram College, Delhi, she obtained her Masters in History from Jawaharlal Nehru University, and later a Masters in English Literature from Allahabad University.

Her translations, articles and book reviews have been published in, among others, *The Illustrated Weekly of India*, the *Book Review*, *Social Scientist*, *Mainstream*, the *Sunday Statesman* and *The Times of India*. Her Hindi translations have been published in *Sarika* and *Hans*.

Sara Rai writes in Hindi and English. At present she lives in Melbourne.

THE
GOLDEN WAIST-CHAIN

A Selection of Hindi Short Stories

Translated and Edited
by
Sara Rai

PENGUIN BOOKS

Penguin Books India (P) Ltd., B4/246, Safdarjung Enclave,
New Delhi 110 029, India
Penguin Books Ltd., Harmondsworth, Middlesex, England
Penguin Books USA Inc., 375 Hudson Street, New York,
N.Y.10014 USA
Penguin Books Australia Ltd., Ringwood, Victoria, Australia
Penguin Books Canada Ltd., 10 Alcorn Avenue, Suite 300, Toronto,
Ontario M4V 3B2, Canada
Penguin Books (NZ) Ltd., 182-190 Wairau Road, Auckland 10, New Zealand

This translation first published by Penguin Books India (P) Ltd. 1992

Copyright © Sara Rai 1990
All rights reserved

Typeset in Palatino by dTech, New Delhi
Made and printed in India by Ananda Offset Private Ltd., Calcutta

For my father, Sripat Rai

CONTENTS

CONTENTS

INTRODUCTION

To select a total of no more than fifteen short stories from the mass of Hindi writing in recent times is a formidable task. No such collection can claim to be representative. Any anthology of this kind must ultimately reflect the editor's personal preferences. But even within the confines of the stories I have liked, there has been a need to be ruthlessly selective. It may be useful, therefore, to outline some of the other criteria that have been involved in making the selection of stories presented here.

First, I decided to limit myself to stories written after Indian Independence in 1947. The stories are thus spread over four decades and explore a good deal of the Indian experience. The best of them represent, as one would expect, much more than that. Good literature, though it belongs to particular contexts, speaks to us, nevertheless, in a universal voice, and the non-Indian reader will, I think, find, perhaps with surprise, much in these stories that is familiar.

At least half a dozen stories are by writers who have been associated with the *Nai Kahani*, or New Story, that emerged as a recognizable form in the Fifties. The years immediately after Partition and Independence were years of high expectation and considerable change. This changing world demanded and produced new ways of 'seeing' and writing. The mood was one of impatience with obsolete social norms. Extricating itself from the mode of romantic idealism adopted by some of the best writers of the previous generation, who mirrored in this some of the aspirations of the anti-colonial struggle, the New Story of the Fifties and after felt the need to draw the reader's attention to other problems and conditions by focusing on new characters and situations.

As Nirmal Verma, one of the best known Hindi writers today, puts it: the New Story 'attempted to touch those rough, harsh and nameless things' that the new world had brought. There was a concern for the genuineness of experience and an insistence on individual awareness and feeling.

Writing by women acquired a clear form in the post-Independence Hindi literary scene and I have felt it necessary to include some of it in this small collection. I have also found it important to make a place for Muslim writers in the anthology. As many Hindu writers were among the distinguished writers of Urdu prose and poetry in the past, today Hindi fiction can boast of an array of powerful Muslim writers; giving the lie to the communal argument that these languages are tied to particular religions.

Far too often a translator is reluctant to break away from the original story and ultimately produces a very literal translation which, though accurate, stumbles along, a captive to the unaccustomed diction of a foreign tongue. I have been on my guard against this while translating the stories. My effort has been to create, in their own right, English versions of the stories. Hindi is in some respects a very extravagant language. Often several adjectives are used in one breath to convey the same image. I have been compelled to hack away some of this undergrowth, for it is my endeavour to be faithful not to the text alone but also to the economy of the English language. If I have not been totally successful in this, I can only apologize to my readers.

This consideration has, to some extent, circumscribed the selection of the stories as well. There are many excellent stories that do not easily lend themselves to translation, being embedded in a very specific context that can only lose colour in a translation. Despite this process of sifting less 'translatable' stories, I have been unable to avoid preparing a glossary for the text, to explain distinctively Indian concepts that are difficult to express in English. It is true that generic terms could well have been used but not without the risk of robbing the story of something nameless but vital. Some beautiful stories have had to be left out of the collection simply because they are too long.

I have preferred to stick to Hindi words to define relationships. Language grows in a social context and since Indian society is in many ways defined by familial ties, Hindi, as also many other Indian languages, is very exacting with regard to forms of address. For instance, *Bua*, *Chachi* and *Khala* do not translate as Aunt; nor do *Dadi* and *Dada* simply mean Grandmother and Grandfather.

*

For me, one of the most moving stories in this collection is Nirmal Verma's 'The Guest'. It deals with human loneliness and alienation and is remarkable for its sensitive characterization and feeling for detail. Though associated with the New Story movement, Nirmal Verma continues to be prolific. This story was written in 1988.

Veering away from the old mood of idealism, Mohan Rakesh's story, titled 'Married Women', depicts the loneliness and adversity faced by two married women, both belonging to different social classes but who share the experience of being used by their husbands. The story makes an implicit statement against the institution of marriage, while it simultaneously probes the less explored layers of human psychology.

Usha Priyamvada's 'The Homecoming' portrays the breakup of the traditional joint family and it is an account that rings true. But sometimes one can feel the writer losing the advantage of distance from her characters, thereby situating the story precariously on the brink of self-pity.

The anthology includes a story, 'The Fire', by Gajanan Madhav Muktibodh, who is better known as a poet. The story is an effort to penetrate the wordless gloom that shrouds Indian middle-class living. It represents not just a quest for self identity but also an intangible dream for integrating the middle class, beset as it is by self-deception, frustration and despair. Highly introspective, the story is in the form of an eternal dialogue that the protagonist conducts with his own self, in an attempt to get very personal answers to existential questions. Perhaps the protagonist is Muktibodh himself.

As a sort of rejoinder to the 'inwardness' of much that was being written in the Fifties and Sixties, Amarkant's 'The City of Death' rehabilitates social responsibility as a creative value. The story is about tension between the Hindu and Muslim communities and the consequent dehumanization of individuals. The issue is one that has acquired grim proportions in much of contemporary Indian living. In a very realistic story, Amarkant gives an optimistic twist to an otherwise depressing situation.

Edging its way outside society, on its lowest fringes, Shrikant Verma's 'The Funeral Procession' firmly establishes the prostitute as a human being just as worthy of love as anybody else. The relationship between a prostitute and a *mehtar*, traditionally on the lowest rung of the Indian social ladder, remains delicately poised on the edge of possibility. The story has an unusual and rather wistful ending.

The anthology also contains 'The Parting' by Zahra Rai and 'The Colour Blue' by Vijay Chauhan. Both these writers have remained relatively unknown. Though they deal with very different sets of circumstances, the two stories share something. It is almost as though life has been surprised in the very act of living, so unobtrusive is the narration. The power of suggestion works very effectively and the stories reverberate with the force of what is left unsaid. The taut economy of the style works on the sensibilities to create effects that would have been impossible to achieve had details been piled one on top of another. For instance, the analogy between fading colour and the sadness inherent in life in 'The Colour Blue' is so subtle as to be almost missed till it strikes all at once with doubled strength.

Ramkumar's 'The Steamer' is written in a controlled, deceptively simple style. It is, in a sense, a story of a modern woman who, breaking away from traditional ties of home, awakens to a yearning for distant horizons. This is a different woman, indeed, from the traditional one whose place is in a private domestic world, where emotions and personal relationships are the focus of moral value and the core of a woman's experience. Yet, as happens so often in life, for the protagonist it is an awakening to limitations. The sparing use of images and the restrained symbolism in the story has the cumulative effect of much achieved with little effort.

Ramnarayan Shukla's 'The Acquaintance' has a similar quality of deliberate simplicity. The note of wistfulness strikes a common chord with 'The Steamer'.

'Apprehension' by Kunwar Narayan is placed, to a greater extent than the other stories, at a level of abstraction. The entire experience of the story is lived within the writer's own peculiar mental landscape and is not linked to external objects or incidents. The reader is not lured into the magic of a story but is asked to stay awake and carry on a debate with himself. Incident and character are placed almost geometrically in order to resolve an increasingly difficult situation. Of course, the effort is ultimately abandoned, as though futile. Nevertheless, it constitutes the mainstay of the story; a story that visibly moves towards the form of an essay or a poem.

'Paper Bullets' by Abdul Bismillah and 'The Festival' by Mehrunnisa Parvez open a window onto the life of impoverished Muslims in India. 'Paper Bullets' is the more recent of the two. Touching little details are worked in very carefully into 'The Festival', demonstrating that, for the feudal class of Muslims fallen upon bad days, a life of dignity and meaning is all but within reach.

Of all the stories in the collection, Sanjeev's 'Traffic Jam' and 'The Golden Waist-Chain', by Uday Prakash, are the most recent. Apart from the fact that 'Traffic Jam' focuses on an almost daily occurrence in modern urban life, a point of interest in the story is the apparent paradox between the static situation inherent in a traffic jam and the sense of seething life that emerges at the actual scene of action. A cross-section of Indian society is on view.

Perhaps the most fascinating story in the collection, for me, is 'The Golden Waist-Chain'. It makes intricate use of folk tradition to produce a highly evocative narrative. The density of images that constitutes the lyrical structure of the prose wages a silent war with the inexorable violence of the plot, the result being a story rich in texture and meaning. The almost objective perspective of the child through whose mouth the story is told, strips the story of moral and social camouflage, and one emerges from the experience a little shaken, haunted by whispering myths.

*

I gratefully acknowledge the generosity of the many writers who have given permission for their stories to be translated and published in this collection.

I owe special thanks to Arvind Krishna Mehrotra for reading through many of these translations and making valuable suggestions for improvement; to Gyan Pandey and Alok Rai for their helpful comments. Nirmal Verma gave some useful suggestions about the translation of his story 'The Guest'.

I need to thank Asad Zaidi and Nasira Sharma for making their rich collections of Hindi fiction available to me. Sharat Chandra Sharma considerably simplified my task of preparing the manuscript by lending me the use of his computer. Ravi Srivastava performed impossible feats with the computer and held in check its errant behaviour. Without their help, my work would have taken much longer. I thank them for giving me their time so generously.

Lara showed extreme consideration by restraining her impulse to tinker with the computer keys and amusing herself elsewhere while I was busy. Aslam was almost as involved with the translations as I was. Without his unfailing support the book would not have been possible.

Finally, I wish to thank Thomas Weber, who started it all.

January 1992   *Sara Rai*

THE FIRE
Gajanan Madhav Muktibodh

She woke up heavy-hearted. She'd had an annoying dream but she now had only a dim memory of the people in it who had pulled faces at her, either openly or behind her back. The entire world had settled on her like a ton of bricks, as indeed it did now.

She looked at the door in front which was still shut. She could hear sounds of coughing from behind it. They came from her aged mother and father-in-law. There was no sound from the other room. Obviously no one was up yet to make the tea. After some time she heard the clink of cups and saucers from the next room. She felt fine now. But this pleasure was short-lived. The moment she realized it was her husband making the tea, a black, acidic gutter began to flow through her heart, reaching a point at which the memory of an incident was inscribed; the image of a person. A man she would once have given her life for. He'd changed now. Her husband.

She got up quickly. Her heart full of venom, she shook the child who slept next to her roughly. She wanted him to cry out, go on screaming, making such a din that every body—her mother and father-in-law, her husband, her elder son (who was studying for a Bachelor of Science degree and had no time for her), the younger brood, would all get disturbed, and, made restless by this harsh crying, would join in the lament. This was the form that her revenge took—her furious revenge that would find its medium in a third person.

She rose from the bed. Running a hand through her hair, she entered the kitchen. Her husband sat on his haunches quietly making the tea. A frail little boy, perhaps three years old, sat naked near him. The older child stood near the tap, filling up the tank with buckets of water.

Rain pelted down, the drops falling haphazardly. Two children, one of whom was asthmatic, had gone off to school without woollens, and without carrying umbrellas. She herself often suffered from bronchitis. Yet, unmindful of herself or the children, she opened the tightly shut kitchen window.

From beyond the blue hills visible in the distance and the grey expanse of the swiftly rippling lake that stretched on for several furlongs, the stormy wind, bending the trees before it, rushed into the kitchen. The room grew wet with the drops the wind carried in.

The husband, who had been watching the boiling tea, shifted his gaze to his unkempt wife. He was stunned. He suddenly realized that he would be called upon to combat various complicated situations today. His mind flipped over the pages of his past life, while he continued to pour tea into the cups, telling the children that this cup was for *Dada* and that one for *Dadi*.

The fine drops fell on his bare back and he could feel one end of his dhoti getting wet. He tried to shut the window to keep out the rain. As he turned to shut the new planks that had been hammered on to the old frame of the window, his eyes were riveted to the horizon where sunbeams from the east were attacking the dim, ashen clouds. The shore of the lake was lost in a blue-grey mist, but the possibility of a ruddy glow presented itself over the green treetops glimmering in the water.

Gazing at the scene spreading into the distance, he stood motionless. Its cool freshness banished the gloom from his heart, replacing it with a strange dancing rhythm.

However, he remained thoughtful. He forced himself to shut the window and settled the children in the kitchen. Holding a cup of tea in his hand, he sat down on the metal chair near the table. He sipped his tea and ruminated over the view from the window.

He felt a sense of continuity with his own past and realized that man's life constituted the process of history; thus he could never be distinct from it. This was as true of his public life, one that he led with others in the external world, as it was of the private, reflective world of his thoughts. This private world was expressed in dreams, through opinions and conclusions. And he had a right to his introspection, particularly if the events of his public life did not force him to emerge from it. Of course, there were those who could not remain thus preoccupied, their external life making more compelling demands on them.

Was it not true that there was a hypothetical figure too in mathematics, something he had learnt while studying for his

Master's degree? Was this hypothetical figure obsolete? Didn't the delicate processes of nature conform to that figure? Was the negative figure just a mathematical unit, an illusory thing? Was not the straight line a special form of the crooked one? Was it a fallacy that one day science and technology would make so much progress that man would be able to use the forces of nature much more effectively than today, and thus change himself? That problematic questions of today, having passed into history, would seem comic, as worthy of laughter as the wars of Rana Dhang, the king of Bundela? Was it not true that a hundred years from now man would become so knowledgeable that he would be able to use new scientific facilities to discuss metaphysical questions? Yes, a hundred years constituted just a moment in the life of the world. History blinked once and a hundred years went by. There was nothing to it! His grandchildren would definitely see that new radiance. Perhaps it would come even earlier. I don't care, he thought. I will live in my dreams. This is my private world and I am entitled to live in it. I am not prepared to let others destroy it!

He finished his tea and put on his kurta absent-mindedly. He could have done with another cup of hot tea, but just then his bent old mother came coughing and spluttering into the room. Her head was a tangled jungle of grey hair, her shrunken body dark and bloodless.

'Can I have another cup of hot tea, Chunnu?' she pleaded.

Pain stabbed at Chunnu's heart when she talked like that. There had been the old days when she had ruled over the entire house! Today her fortunes had changed and she had to beg for a cup of tea. Wasn't it his duty to provide for this frail asthma-ridden form? But he had no idea how he would do that. But for the two spoons of milk he had saved up for his wife, there was none left. What was he supposed to do now?

He held his mother in a gaze and guffawed suddenly. He clasped her in his arms, gripping her so tightly that she squirmed with pain. 'Let go, Chunnu! Let go!' Paying no heed, he waltzed around the room with her, almost lifting her off the ground. Eight-year-old Babua clapped, enjoying the spectacle while three-year-old Bundu stood up to get a better look. Then the eight-year-old made off to apprise his irate mother of the performance that was in progress. Not very clever of him, for the terrace adjacent to the kitchen, where the children's mother had wandered off, began to emit fumes of angry fire. She was obviously not in a good mood today.

Suddenly, Chunnu was flinging around his papers in a frenzy; the papers that he had nurtured so lovingly. The place looked a mess with all that paper scattered about. The eight-year-old child was in charge of reorganizing the paper, a responsibility he shouldered with great determination. The situation was soon under control and the little bundles of paper had been housed in a large bag. The papers were newspaper scraps, exercise books the children no longer used, pages carrying news from Russian and American agencies and from old issues of *New Times* and *Newsweek* that he now had no use for.

A little later, bag slung carelessly over his shoulder, Chunnilal-Sharma, alias Chunnu, M.Sc., Assistant Teacher, climbed down the stairs flanking the room, hoping to slip out of the house without his wife noticing. She looked angry today and he dreaded having to confront her early in the morning!

However, the fear proved baseless. The coast was quite clear. As was customary with him, the sparkling freshness of the morning conjured up dreams before his eyes. He saw his children grown-up. They had all turned out to be industrious and clever too. Their clothes were in tatters, it was true. Nonetheless, they wove Kant, Marx, Sartre and Nehru into their speeches with enviable ease. With fiery enthusiasm they strove towards the golden ideal. Better times were ahead and the present generation seemed almost comic in its traditionalism. These were Chunnu's dreams.

Meanwhile, the children's mother had made some tea for herself. It was black, the two spoons of milk notwithstanding. She felt better however. The hot tea travelled down her throat, bringing her back to life. Her gaze strayed to the window she had earlier opened. Somebody had shut it. She got up in disgust and pushed it open again.

The newly risen sun cast a rosy hue over the sky. Spreading outward from a focal point, the sunbeams had chased the clouds away to the west and the lake was suffused with their gentle radiance. The green field was aflame with the red and gold but the hill in the distance was a blue triangle.

She gazed at the scene wistfully, her face aglow with its beauty. She set a bucket under a tap in the room and sat down near the stove, her eyes fixed on the red embers. Scarlet mountains grew up in them, translucent and golden. Little lanes of fine, warm ash formed a white labyrinth near the mountains. Wispy tendrils of fire waved out, as though beckoning to someone they loved.

Flames danced out over the stove as she replenished it with firewood. A rhythm of movement, a passionate energy was being created; it was the birth of the sun's progeny! She cast a joyful look around the kitchen. The brass utensils arranged on the wooden planks on the wall glittered, their gold mingling with the rose of the riotous sun.

Her eyes travelled to her bangles; a blue circle of light enclosed her wrist. As if in response to some indefinable impulse, she abruptly touched her forehead to the bangles, as though bowing to an unseen force. A dream swam in her eyes, flitting across her lips in a smile. The fire gained strength. Red and rust, vermilion and gold rose higher; dancing, waving.

She had put nothing on the stove. Warmth and light surged out as she adjusted the firewood in it. Her mind raced back to the past, trying to recollect the event of the day before. What was the incident that had consumed her spirit, thrown her into a frenzy? Try as she would, she could remember nothing. Perhaps there had been no such incident at all. The toxins generated by her unhealthy body had left her weak and susceptible to these delusions. Self-destructive thoughts floated inside her, vitiating her state of mind and threatening to gnaw away her insides.

Yet, gazing into that valley of fiery golden blossoms, visions from her lost childhood and youth stole upon her and she felt a pang for those wasted years which she could have spent in studying towards a vocation. That woman would not then have come surreptitiously to her backdoor; the one who took more interest than even the Pathan, and she would have been saved her humiliation.

She remembered her friends who had finished studying and now had jobs as clerks, teachers or nurses. A consciousness of deprivation and inadequacy gripped her as the sordid misery of her life flashed before her. A child every other year, the cycle of birth and death, humiliating debts, mounting responsibilities, the fight against hunger, and above all else, the relentless drudgery of work.

It was surprising that she did not once think of her husband in all this. It wasn't even the case that she felt no antagonism towards him, but the case that, in spite of it all, she loved him dearly. She could never for a moment have conceived of blaming him for her troubles, though it was true that he often suffered the brunt of her frustration. Man's heart is strange indeed. Given the fact that she was so angry with her husband today, she should certainly have felt hostile towards him. However, she held her lack of formal education responsible for her present condition.

She would have been better off had she been educated for she certainly considered herself worldly-wise, compared to her husband. He possessed the power to infuse the heart with an innocent joy but she was aware that he lacked the strength of will that was necessary to meet life's struggle. As she saw it, her husband could be classified a saint; she would never have called him a simpleton, far less thought him one.

Absorbed in her thoughts, the wild-haired woman noticed nothing when an ember flew up from the stove and hid itself in a fold of her sari.

At precisely this point, her husband, Chunnilal, was at a grubby grocery store, contemplating the picture of a woman printed on a nondescript yellow packet of tea that he had found on a shelf. His eyes travelled over the woman's dusky face and the basket of flowers she clasped in her hand, contrasting strangely with her wide open dark eyes. The presence of the woman's picture seemed quite inexplicable to him.

He picked up a grimy scrap of newspaper from the floor and spread it out on a sticky stool before perching himself on it. Rummaging silently in his shoulder bag, he began to take out the waste paper it contained. Arithmetic sums worked out in broken crooked letters, names of state capitals and Sanskrit verbs his children had written, fell out of the bag.

He gazed into the future again. Considering that he did not have money for their books, it was hardly likely that his children would go to college. But they would certainly imbibe his philosophy of life. He would see to it that they studied systematically. He would also encourage them to keep at a distance from the wealthy and become realistic enough to live amongst those who were poor like themselves, providing them with new inspiration and insight. They would be revolutionaries living on the brink of society; writing books, printing pamphlets, sharing their modest resources and despising the sensationalism that had acquired the name of education and culture. . . .

The grocer was none the wiser for all this. All he knew was that waste paper sold at no more than six annas a kilo. The sight of fifteen annas in his hand delighted Chunnilal, and he proceeded at once to a neighbouring teashop to buy some milk.

There was bedlam at home. The children were weeping and so was his old mother, her dark wrinkles trembling and wet with tears. Deathly shadows played across his father's face as he splashed buckets of water on Chunnu's wife who lay prone on the floor. She was soaked to the skin. Blisters of dry mud had risen up on the parched floor where the water had not seeped in evenly. The noise of uproarious weeping burst through the roof and poured out of the window, but at the heart of the tumult was a deep silence, in which his wife lay shrouded.

The woman lay stunned, her peevishness having fled with the wind. The incident had obviously left a deep impression on her. She was unable to understand why the fire had attacked her. Buckets of water were poured on the fire. Her sari and the sweater underneath it had emerged very much the worse for wear. People were applying blue ink to her burns. It was probably the children's luck that the fire did not spread too far. The woman still lay there silently, wild-eyed and completely passive. It was difficult to gauge her thoughts. The old parents stood by, pathetic in their guilt. Their presence somehow accentuated the poverty of Chunnu's home, and now their minds were pitiful too.

Chunnu stepped forward, shouldering the responsibility. He flung shyness to the wind and shook the motionless woman's head in an attempt to make her sit up. She did sit up, and, finding her husband before her, lowered her eyes in embarrassment, for there were others watching her too.

Chunnu became aware that he would now have to emerge from the private world he inhabited, to jump into the fray and take matters into his hands. He could shelve his dreams for the time being for he would need all the skill he could muster to bring circumstances under control.

Should he summon Vaidji . . .? . . . Burnol . . . the physician . . .? Incoherent thoughts circled his brain, but pushing all else into the background was the one overriding anxiety—medical attention for his wife would require money and where was that going to come from? The fact that he was in need of help hurt his pride, though he could not get the idea out of his mind.

It stayed there, beating relentlessly, like a drum.

When he examined his wife's back more closely, however, he realized that the burns—he counted six, of different sizes and shapes—did not warrant the attention of a physician; Burnol would set them right. Leaving his wife where she was, he set off on a neighbour's bicycle to buy some.

The pall of gloom had lifted. Though the woman still lay in quiet resignation, a little child now played on his mother's outstretched legs while the older child conscientiously applied blue ink to her burns; the old mother had retired from the scene. Chunnu returned and sat down near his wife, his gaze searching her transfixed, unseeing eyes. He touched her cheek lightly and found that recognition had returned to her eyes and a soft smile curved her lips. He felt an upsurge of self-pity. It was his ill-luck that he saw people around him in the garb of characters from a novel, who, though extremely close to the writer, may still be but shadows.

He pulled the woman close, nevertheless. Just then she spoke in a feeble voice, 'Don't leave me alone!' The voice seemed to come to Chunnilal from the farthest shore, with a heart-rending poignance acquired on the way. He laid his wife on the ground, with a wooden plank under her head to serve as a pillow. Overcome with agitation, he opened the kitchen window and gazed outside. An imaginary world composed of towns and villages, lanes and alleyways grew up before his unseeing eyes, and an echo seemed to rise from their depths: 'Don't leave me alone!'

Meanwhile, his mother crouched motionless in the kitchen, as though in a stupor. The stove was still ablaze. Chunnilal set the kettle on it for tea. As he handed out the cups of tea, the wan faces of his children, his father's wrinkles and the fading irises of his mother's eyes seemed to beseech him, 'Don't leave us alone!'

When he'd made the tea, he found his wife asleep. As he tried to wake her up, his eyes encompassed the scene. The little child still played on his mother's knees. The three-year-old had busied himself with counting the pieces of chalk in his pocket. Keeping office and school timings in mind and given the situation in the house, the older boy was trying to help out with the morning meal by scanning the dal for particles of grit. Blue ink stained his hands, looking as though he'd been playing with the ink-pot.

The poignance of the scene moved Chunni. In containing his love for his family, his heart felt like an earthenware pot that would burst if filled any further. His glance travelled over the house that was his entire world. It was his duty to serve his family; a duty he would certainly not shirk. There alone lay the meaning of his life.

He decided not to wake his wife up, and, instead, gave the cup of tea to his father. He slowly sipped his own tea, but it had scarcely touched his lips when he remembered that he hadn't applied Burnol to his wife's blisters. He put the cup down and a troubling thought came to his mind—why had he forgotten the Burnol? He tried to grapple with this question, which, at this point, seemed to hold a very personal meaning. It was time for him to establish a relationship with the external world, with his work, and not solely with the intangible world of feeling he had so far inhabited. Just then the older child announced, 'Mother wants some tea.'

Chunnu was happy. Handing a cup of tea to his wife, he made himself comfortable near her. As the children watched, their grandfather, bent with age, handed over the tube of Burnol to their father.

THE ACQUAINTANCE
Ramnarayan Shukla

My acquaintance with Ghosh *Babu* goes back to when I was fifteen or sixteen. I had got my matriculation results ten days before. I wanted to take up science for further study but could not get admission anywhere on account of my low marks. *Chacha* was concerned about my admission too. It was on his suggestion that I had decided to study science. Rather than simply setting up shop, he would have liked me to be a doctor or an engineer.

Chacha returned from the shop one night and said to me, 'Come to the shop tomorrow morning at ten o'clock, Amal. I've arranged to get you admitted to the I.S.C.'

I was very pleased to hear this. I had spent the last ten days floundering in an effort to gain admission to a college but had drawn a blank everywhere. Given the circumstances, I broke into a broad smile when *Chacha* gave me this information.

I reached the shop at ten o'clock sharp the next morning. *Chacha* was talking to a gentleman inside. When he saw me, he said, 'Look, Amal, go along with this gentleman. He knows someone in H.R. College. He'll see to it that you get admitted there.'

The gentleman talked about many things to me in the tram. He asked me several questions too. How old was I? What plans did I have for my future? Which school had I matriculated from? And many others. In the course of the conversation, even without my asking, he told me about himself too. He had a son who studied in the ninth class. He had a daughter who was married seven or eight years back and was now comfortably settled. His wife had died. He lived in a rented room in Maulali with his son. He'd owned a shop two years ago but had to sell it off for lack of capital. He had spent the last two years supplying goods to people on board ships docked at the port. There were many other things he told me but that is all I remember today.

He knew a clerk at the college who somehow talked the principal into admitting me.

I did not see him again for five years. He appeared quite suddenly one afternoon when I was sitting in the shop. As soon as he entered, I thought I'd seen him somewhere, though I could not remember where and under what circumstances. He caught me staring at him and said, 'Don't you remember me? I'm the person who got you admitted into college!'

'Yes, of course!' I said, springing to my feet. 'Please do take a seat!' He sat down on the chair before him while I remained standing.

He produced a grimy handkerchief from his pocket and wiped his face. Then he ran a glance around the shop and remarked, 'I can't see Punno *Babu* anywhere.'

'*Chacha's* gone out.'

'Where to?' he gave a start. 'Has he gone off to the village?'

'No, sir, he's certainly in Calcutta. He's just gone out for a couple of hours on work.'

He sat transfixed for a while when he heard that. Then, after some thought, he asked, 'How did you fare with your studies?'

'I failed the I.S.C. once, but managed to pass the next year with a second division. I took the B.Sc. examination this year but I failed. There's no hope I'll pass the next year either. That is why I've decided it's best to attend to the shop.' I got all this out in one breath.

He said nothing. Suddenly I remembered what he had told me five years ago. 'Isn't your son in his fourth year at college now?' I asked him as I did a mental calculation.

'He failed last year,' he said very softly. 'He's passed this year with a second division. I've got him admitted into college just ten or twelve days ago.'

Just then a customer came into the shop and engaged me in conversation. He scrutinized various kinds of cigars for close to fifteen minutes then left after buying a packet of Burma cigars. Meanwhile, Ghosh *Babu* sat in quiet contemplation. When the customer had gone, he looked at me and said, 'Well, I need some supplies too. I'm in a hurry.'

'What kind of supplies?' I asked, a little surprised.

He dug out a scrap of paper from his pocket. Consulting it, he asked me for a couple of packets of cigars and seven or eight different kinds of cigarettes. It took me some time to work out what he wanted and in how much quantity. I asked him to repeat what he'd said. At this, he handed me the scrap of paper and said, 'I'd like all the cigars and cigarettes mentioned here.'

I took the slip from his hand. It had other things on it too, apart from cigars and cigarettes. I took out the things he had asked for and put them in the large bag he'd brought with him.

I had begun to sit in the shop only very recently. That was why *Chacha* had given me a price-list written in a thin exercise book which I could use as and when the situation demanded. I added up the prices of all that he had bought and handed the piece of paper to him. The total was forty-five rupees and a few annas.

He examined the slip of paper carefully for a few minutes before asking, 'How did you calculate these prices?'

'I've written the price we sell at,' I retorted quickly. He laughed softly, then smiled and said, 'You haven't taken me for a regular customer, have you? I'm only taking all this stuff to sell it. You've forgotten that I told you I supplied goods to ships.'

'What then?' I enquired after some thought.

'Punno *Babu* gives me everything at only a few annas over the cost price. He would take barely thirty-seven or thirty-eight rupees from me for all of this.'

A customer entered just then and started talking to me. He was in the shop for about five minutes but left without purchasing anything. In the meantime Ghosh *Babu* had taken some money out of his pocket. He placed this in my hand when the customer left, with the words, 'Here are thirty-five rupees. Keep them and give the list of the things I took to Punno *Babu*. I'll drop in tomorrow morning and pay whatever balance he wishes to charge me.' Seeing that I had no objection to this, he left.

I kept regular hours at the shop now. It was usual for Ghosh *Babu* to visit the shop at least once or twice a fortnight, either to replenish his stock of goods or simply to take a little break. His age had begun to show. He had looked quite different when I first saw him—seven years ago. He seemed to have aged about twenty years since then.

I had been sitting at the shop for two years now and was experienced enough not to have to consult the price-list to sell things. I understood the business rather well, I thought. I could rattle off the retail prices of all the goods. Normally it was our practice to sell every thing with a profit margin of fifteen to twenty per cent. In keeping with *Chacha*'s instructions, I took a profit of only three or four per cent from Ghosh *Babu*.

Ghosh *Babu* looked tired when he came into the shop one day. He sat down on a chair at once. When I asked him something, he just waved at me to be silent. I stood looking at him quietly. He was quite out of breath. It was almost twenty minutes before he moved from that position. Then he asked me for a drink of water. I got him a glass of water from the next shop. His panting stemmed a little when he'd had the drink. Handing back the glass to me he explained, 'It's a respiratory ailment. It just won't leave me in peace.' He smiled wanly as he said, 'There's no way it is going to let me alone now. . . it will accompany me to my deathbed! Well, that's not too far now either!'

'Don't talk like that!' I said, trying to console him. 'You're doing fine. And you're not so very old yet anyway. . . !'

'I don't get to see Punno *Babu* much these days,' he changed the topic himself. 'Doesn't he come here at all now?'

'These days he is in the village.'

He stared at the floor silently. He'd been here for almost forty-five minutes. This was the longest he had ever sat in the shop. I gazed at him sitting like that for a while. Then I remembered his son. 'Is your son well?' I asked him after thinking a while. An expression of contentment flitted across his face; he liked talking about his son.

'His result will be out soon. He's just taken his B.A. final examination—he's sure to land some job or the other if he passes it,' he told me proudly.

At this point a customer entered the shop and seeing that I was busy, Ghosh *Babu* left.

He came one morning when I was opening the shop at nine o'clock. This was the first time he'd come so early. I gave him a smile, 'You're very early today?'

'There's no knowing when one will be called out in this profession, son. It can be at ten o'clock in the morning or eleven at night!' he sounded annoyed. 'A customer has demanded some things at this early hour, and, if I'm late, he won't deal with me tomorrow. Really, I think you're much better off with your own shop. At least you can keep the hours that suit you and the customers simply have to adjust accordingly . . . .'

I noticed that he had become rather irritable of late. His son had passed with a second division and he had been worrying about a job for him for the past six months. So far all his efforts had failed. 'What's your son up to these days?' I asked him, just casually.

'He is busy writing applications the whole day; what else can the poor fellow do?' There seemed to be a lump in his throat when he reached the last sentence.

'Why don't you ask him to help you out till he gets fixed up with something?' I was certain he would approve of my suggestion. 'It's not right for you to slog like this at your age. Surely he could give you a hand while he's waiting for a job?'

'Assist me in my work?' he said in an unfamiliar voice. 'Do you have any idea what my work involves?'

'Well yes,' I said, though his voice worried me a little. 'You supply goods to ships. You told me so yourself!'

'Yes, I know I did. . . ,' his voice had acquired a note of aggression, 'but I didn't give my son an education so that he should go around selling things from a bag!'

What he said made me a little angry. I gave it some thought and then said, 'Well, to begin with, there could be nothing wrong with whatever one does by the sweat of one's brow. If you think differently, you're mistaken. *Chacha* didn't want me to sit in this shop either.'

The stand that I had taken obviously worried him. 'No, it's nothing like that,' he said. 'I spoke without thinking. You are still a child and I find it difficult to explain things to you. Punno *Babu* had come up with the same suggestion a few days ago. Ask him about it if you can.'

Having said this he went away. I spent the entire day thinking about him. I made up my mind to find an opportune moment to ask about him, though I was not in the habit of gossiping with *Chacha*. I was on the verge several times, but somehow the words stuck in my throat. He disliked inane talk. He would certainly consider my questions trivial.

It was Sunday, a day we usually spent at home. The shop was closed. We occupied two rooms. I had lived with *Chacha* in Calcutta for the last ten years. *Amma* lived with my young brothers and sisters in the village. *Chacha* didn't marry. On Sundays it was customary for him to be home till about four in the afternoon. He went out after that, and came home again by nine or ten o'clock.

It started to rain that afternoon at about half past three. *Chacha* sat at the window staring out at the rain till five o'clock. Restlessness was clearly visible on his face. He got up constantly to peer out of the window. I had borrowed a novel from the shop in front the day before and was supposed to return it the next morning. I had been reading it since ten in the morning and finished it around five o'clock. I put it away and glanced at *Chacha*. He lay with his eyes closed. I went and stood near him, staring at his face for a long time.

I thought he looked tired and quite run-down. Just then he opened his eyes and was startled to see me. I got a start as well. He had caught me looking at him; his eyes registered a complaint. I thought I shouldn't have stood so close to him. 'What is the matter?' he asked gravely.

'No, it's nothing. . . ,' I stammered.

He lay silently for some time. I was in a strange frame of mind. I didn't quite know what I should do. After thinking a little, he said, 'Did you want to ask me something? Go ahead. Is it about the shop?'

'Last night Ghosh *Babu* paid five rupees too little,' I lied in an effort to produce an immediate answer. *Chacha* had gone away from the shop at seven o'clock the previous evening. I had closed for the night at half past eight. Ghosh *Babu* had come after *Chacha* left. He had bought goods worth about twenty-five rupees and had paid the full amount. Since I was supposed to open the shop the next morning, I thought I'd tell *Chacha* later that Ghosh *Babu* had been in to pay the balance.

'Oh, don't worry about that. It doesn't matter. He's a good man.' The lines of worry were fading from *Chacha*'s face. We sat in silence for some time. It was still raining outside. The roof dripped in a couple of places. When it began to drip on the spot where *Chacha* sat, he moved closer to me.

'What kind of work does he do?' I asked him just then.

'Who?' he asked, a little startled.

'Ghosh *Babu*.'

'Why, he supplies goods to ships.'

I was aware of this myself and the brief reply disappointed me a little. Then an idea struck me—by asking him the question I'd thought of, he would be sure to tell me if there was any thing wrong with the kind of work Ghosh *Babu* did. 'Wouldn't it be good if we could do the same work too? I asked with deliberation. 'It would be an added source of income these days when the shop isn't doing too well.'

'Which work do you mean?'

'The kind that Ghosh *Babu* does.'

'Certainly not. That's no work for us.' *Chacha* looked worried at what I had said. 'It's not an easy task, trying to get round people—you'd tire yourself cajoling them. Then there are all kinds of things they ask for; some of them are difficult to come by.'

'Well, there are problems with any thing one does . . . ,' I said after a little consideration. 'Do you really think running our shop is simple?'

'Don't you see? Our problems are quite different,' admonished *Chacha*. 'We aren't capable of bootlicking. Really, it's absurd. . . you can be asked to produce anything . . . from flowers to liquor. Running from pillar to post is not my idea of a good job!'

I shut up when I heard this. I would have liked to clarify many other things with him but *Chacha* had averted his face. I knew he'd flare up at any further questions.

Rain was pelting down, gaining in force as the darkness intensified. *Chacha*'s face grew restless when he glanced out of the window or carefully around the room. He sat quietly for some time. Water was dripping onto my clothes. There was no spot left where we could sit without getting wet. 'It's rained like this for the first time after 1947. . . ,' said *Chacha*, his eyes on the wet floor.

I chose to say nothing to this. An ancient memory floated in my eyes . . . the fifteenth of August, 1947. I was very little then, studying in Class Four at the village school. The people at the school were jubilant! I still remembered the festivity there'd been! There were many other things I remembered about that day. 'Was Calcutta very festive?' I asked thoughtfully.

'Festive? What kind of festivity?'

Chacha's question astonished me. 'Why, to celebrate that we were free at last!'

A strange smile flitted across *Chacha*'s face. A strong wind had risen outside and the windows banged shut or were flung open. I thought *Chacha* would say something; perhaps narrate an incident relating to Independence Day. However, he said nothing.

I stared out of the window contemplatively. I like rain, particularly when it is accompanied by a strong wind. A tranquil environment doesn't attract me. Often it's so lonely within, that one appreciates a turbulent exterior.

'You must admit we lead a hand-to-mouth existence. Any additional income would be welcome, whatever be its source,' I said, after giving the matter some thought.

'Whatever the source?' *Chacha* started up, 'what do you mean by that?'

'Oh nothing at all!' I said hurriedly, perturbed by his question. 'It's just that I wonder sometimes why we can't supply stuff to ships. I don't think the kind of problems you mention are daunting enough.'

Chacha gazed steadily at my face. His lips trembled. He looked like he had something to say but could not bring himself to do so. I looked quietly at his face noting the many different expressions that flitted quickly across it. A strange loneliness had clouded his eyes.

'I've always found it difficult to tackle stubbornness. I would appreciate it if you left off your obstinacy.' He spoke so softly that I heard him with some effort. 'There are certain things one has to accept without question . . . and there are some that are better left unknown. What will you get by knowing so much?'

His last sentence reminded me of *Pitaji*. I had just a dim memory of him, for he died when I was only seven or eight. When he was home, I remember, he would give me a ride on his back every evening. During this time, he talked to me about all kinds of things. He answered all my questions. Sometimes I asked him so many at once that he got annoyed. 'Why are you so inquisitive?' he would ask. Today, when I remembered those days, all that he'd said flashed across my mind.

I did not see Ghosh *Babu* for a couple of days. It was not a very busy time of the year. Sometimes I spent a whole day in the shop with only a few customers coming in. Many thoughts came to my idle mind.

It was only on the third day that I saw Ghosh *Babu* approaching. He walked with much effort, as though he dragged something heavy behind him. His bag, I noticed when he came closer, was full of things. He made an attempt to smile when he saw me. But the weary lines on his haggard face did not let the smile surface. He came and stood in front of the shop. 'Do sit down!' I said, gesturing towards a chair.

'No, some other time; I'm in a bit of a hurry today. I have to deliver these things to my customers. Can you give me a packet of Ronson flint?'

I handed him a packet of flint. He scrutinized it. Then, after some thought, he said, 'Do you know, Amal, the lighter won't ignite without these little pieces of stone? There can be no light in our lives either if our hearts don't turn to stone. People like us are like lighters without a flint; who won't burn however hard we try.'

I felt a little odd listening to him. Ghosh *Babu* had never spoken like that before. Maybe others were familiar with this side of his but I got a glimpse of it for the first time.

'You asked me why I never ask my son to help me out . . . ,' his voice had acquired the tone of a soliloquy. 'I'm his father. Of course, you can argue that there'd be many fathers who would be happy to use their sons to such a purpose. However, I think that's because they've put this flint where their hearts ought to be . . . .' His voice, becoming lower, faded away.

I studied his face attentively; he appeared quite dejected. I considered asking him about his son but decided against it. I glanced over at the things in the shop. I had never before felt that it was too dark in the shop. I would have to put in more lights.

Suddenly there was a sound of splintering glass. I went outside to check what had broken. An expensive teapot had smashed in the shop next door. Ghosh *Babu* had followed me. We sat down and scrutinized the pieces scattered about. Ghosh *Babu* left soon after.

I ran my eyes along the line of shops. Not many people were about; only the shopkeepers sat in front of their shops. I went back inside. It surprised me to see the packet of flint still on the table. Ghosh *Babu* had obviously forgotten it and would probably be back for it soon.

I came outside again and sat down, convinced that Ghosh *Babu* would be back before it was closing time. Once, long ago, he had left a packet of cigars behind in the same fashion. He had come back for it just when I was preparing to go and I'd had to open up the shop again for him.

I thought about him the whole day. The packet of flint was in my pocket. I had planned to have some fun at his expense if he happened to be in a good mood. I'd pretend I didn't have the packet, and, when he got tired of looking for it, I'd produce it from my pocket! He'd smile a little, or maybe not at all. I had seldom seen him smile.

However, he did not turn up. Contrary to my custom, I shut the shop at nine that night instead of at half past eight. The packet of flint was still in my pocket. Maybe he would arrive just when I was about to close up and go away.

The same feeling persisted the next morning when I opened the shop; I thought he would come right away and sit down inside. I had transferred the flint from my pocket to the table. I had decided to give it to him as soon as he came, but there was no sign of him throughout the day. Though I expected to see him at least when I was closing shop, he did not show up.

Fifteen or twenty days passed. Maybe he was sick. I did not know where he lived. Once, in the course of a conversation, I'd asked him and he told me he lived near Dum Dum. He had even told me the name of the road but I had forgotten it. It would have been difficult to find the house without the number anyway.

Whenever I thought about him, all kinds of visions would come to my eyes. Sometimes I pictured him alone in an extremely dark room, coughing away. There was no one to look after him; perhaps he could not even get up. Even if people wanted to assist him, he was beyond help of any kind. Could he have been in a road accident and was now hospitalized?

The days passed very slowly indeed. The market had not been lucrative at all lately. *Chacha* worried about money all the time. It was tough trying to make ends meet. I thought about my student days often. Those unsuccessful days annoyed me now. Had I been able to obtain a degree, I could have got myself a job and been of some help to my family. *Chacha* had never wanted me to attend to the shop. He had planned to sell off the shop when I finished studying. He had been proud of me. Lost in thought, I sometimes forgot where I was.

Strange dreams haunted me at night. In a recurrent one, I was taking an examination, and, though I knew all the answers, I could write nothing. The hours ran out and I had to leave my examination copy blank. I came out sadly and thought about my copy in which nothing could be written now; there was a time when I could have done so, but didn't. I always woke up at this point.

The days went by. It was two months now since Ghosh *Babu* had left his packet of flint behind. Sometimes the dreaded thought came to me, what if . . . but I did not let the gloom linger for long. Whenever I thought about his death, I felt as though someone was breathing very softly beside me.

I thought about his son often too. I'd never set eyes on him. For some reason I felt I would recognize him though. I started up sometimes and looked at the passers-by carefully to check if he were one of them.

And then one day I saw Ghosh *Babu* approaching. He looked all terrible. Though he held nothing in his hands, one might have thought, by the way he walked, that he carried a heavy load. He came up slowly and stood in front of the shop. His legs trembled. The sight of his hands gave me goose-flesh. They looked like they could not lift even an empty bag.

He stood there, leaning against the showcase, giving the impression that he would fall without it.

'Do come in!' I said, seeing that he did not speak. He entered quietly and sat down on a chair. There were many things I wanted to ask him. Yet, today, when I found him before me, there was not a word I could say. He gazed at the floor sadly while I fumbled for speech.

I remembered the packet of flint just then. I took out a packet from the showcase and put it in his hand. I said, 'There you are! You forgot it here the last time!'

No remembrance stirred on his face.

'You didn't come for so long . . . were you sick?' I asked, slowly, since he said nothing.

'Sick. . . ? Did you think I was sick?' His feeble voice seemed unfamiliar to me.

'Yes! And looking at you now confirms what I thought.' I had expected him to smile back, but he didn't.

'Yes, I was sick, but do you think any kind of sickness could deter me from work? Especially at a time when my son is out of work and walks miles because he can't pay the tram fare?' he said thickly. I thought about his son . . . about that day a year ago when Ghosh *Babu* said his results would be out soon and that he was certain to get a job if he passed.

'I thought about you often,' I said, and remembered all that I had thought.

'Did you? I remembered every thing outside . . . roads, markets, shops, people; wide stretches of field. I feel strange today. When I thought about the world outside, I felt I had left it behind; I'd never see it again. Do you have any idea where I was?' He paused to examine my face. 'I was in jail . . . for two-and-a-half months.'

'In jail?' I said incredulously. This hadn't occurred to me in my wildest thoughts.

'Yes, in jail,' Ghosh *Babu* said in a controlled voice. 'I remember the judge said that the punishment should be protracted and severe, considering the nature of the offence. However, taking into account the poor health and the age of the accused, the sentence was shortened.'

'Offence?' The word escaped my lips and it struck me only later that I shouldn't have said that.

'It's quite usual for an unemployed father to commit some sort of offence. By doing so he postpones the crime his son would commit. I was accused of smuggling. Two bottles of Scotch and three Swiss watches were found in my bag.' Ghosh *Babu* talked completely dispassionately, as though he were discussing a third person.

'Where?' I could not control my curiosity.

'On the steps of the ship.' He spoke as though he were narrating a story. 'Amal, do you remember asking me why I did not let my son help me? I didn't tell you the whole story then. But I'll do so today.'

I listened to him silently. There was no trace of emotion on his face. He did look a little pathetic though. He said, 'Ten years ago I sold my shop because I had no capital. I was out of work too. I tried all avenues for a year. There seemed to be no way out. Then I began to supply goods to ships from the limited resources that I had. It was extremely risky but I had no other option. Often I got foreign watches and liquor as a reward for services rendered and I sold them. Sometimes I got caught. In the last ten years, I've spent eleven months in jail.'

He paused. Then he said as though remembering something he'd forgotten, 'I was finished the day I began this work and knew it . . . My only consolation was that my son would lead a life totally different from mine. It was then that I started paying attention to his studies.'

He told me many more things about his life that day and I still remember them though I do not wish to. I always think of him when I see people in similar situations.

I did not see him again for about fifteen days. In this period his frail body and trembling face often rose before my eyes and I thought about all he had told me.

I was talking to a customer one afternoon when he came by. He carried his bag this time. He came inside the shop when the customer left and sat down. I looked at his bag attentively and noticed that it held something.

'I've managed to borrow about a hundred rupees,' he explained, catching me looking at his bag. 'I'm starting work again today. There is no other way out.' He spoke as though he had to justify himself. I said nothing. I remembered the day when he'd first come to buy his things; when he had laughed and asked me whether I thought he was a customer.

For some time neither of us spoke. The fan sounded strange, whirring away.

'Can I have a packet of Java Dawson cigars?' he asked, looking at the cigars arranged in the showcase. 'A fresh one please. These local cigars tend to get stale because they are badly packed.'

I gave him a packet of cigars and he left. He didn't pay me for it. He said, 'Put it on my account; I'll pay you the next time.'

Now I saw him almost every day. He was so frail he looked like he would stumble and fall when he walked. He changed his bag over to the other hand every two hundred yards, however little it may have had in it. It went on like this for about fifteen days, after which he suddenly stopped coming.

This time I was convinced that he was very sick. Even before, he had been in no condition to walk a couple of hundred yards. I remembered his problems, his son . . . . What had he said about every poor father committing a crime and thereby preventing . . .?

A month passed by and Ghosh *Babu* did not come. I saw him coming one evening when I was talking to a salesman from the shop across the road. He didn't have his bag with him. As he came closer, I noticed that he was followed by a youth of about my age who carried his bag. I realized that this must be his son.

He came up to the shop. The youth stopped in his tracks too. Ghosh *Babu* was quite out of breath. When I saw him, I confirmed my suspicion that he must have been sick. In fact, he looked so weak, I was surprised he could still walk.

'This is my son,' he said, sitting down on a chair. 'Now he'll work instead of me. I've been sick for the past month; I've no strength left.'

I held his son in my gaze. He stood quietly, holding on to Ghosh *Babu*'s bag. All that Ghosh *Babu* had told me flashed through my mind.

'Now you'll see him, not me . . . .' Ghosh *Babu* looked at his son's face reflectively. 'Treat him like a younger brother and help him as much as you can. You know I didn't want this, but . . . .'

THE PARTING
Zahra Rai

The black horse-drawn coach came to a halt before the back gate of the hospital. That gate was often locked. The doors of the carriage were shut. From the window two anxious eyes looked out.

Getting down from the top of the carriage, the driver patted the shining back of the black horse and looked around carefully. Then he opened the doors of the carriage with deference, and, stepping back a little, softly said, 'Madam may alight; there is no one here.'

A tall woman wearing a black burqa stepped out. A thin veil covered her face, through which her translucent fair skin glowed as her restless eyes impatiently took in her surroundings.

There was no path from that gate to the main building of the hospital. It was usual for the patients to use the front gate. Leading from this gate was a cemented road, and, beside this, a lawn, flowers and fountains. The back gate opened on to grounds that were full of grass reaching up to the knees, where innumerable insects hovered.

The visitor negotiated this undergrowth with rapid strides and went into the office of the head nurse. She lifted her veil; her age was twenty-five, perhaps. Beautiful eyes with just a trace of kohl and palms decorated with little orange dots of henna. She asked the nurse in a low voice, 'Is everything ready?'

'Madam, you will have to wait a minute.'

'Can I see her?'

'You will have to wait just a little,' she repeated. She took out some cards from the cupboard and began to fill in various columns. She then stood up, and, turning to the lady, said, 'Please wait here.'

The lady inclined her head slightly. With one hand on the stiff white triangular cap on her head, the nurse went out with quick steps. Her soft shoes made no sound. Her eyes showed little emotion. Just the determination to get through the hours assigned for her duty. She looked at her watch and lowered her wrist. It was four in the afternoon. Another nurse would relieve her at five. At six I am expected at the Plaza, she thought.

The rooms of the private patients lined both sides of the corridor. A middle-aged woman had fainted in one of the rooms. Perhaps there was something wrong with her heart. Her relatives stood by anxiously. All had tense, pursed lips. Two young lady doctors were looking after her. The patient in the adjoining room was happy. She was to be discharged today. A big car stood outside the hospital building, just in front of the room. Children were making a loud racket and there was a general atmosphere of merriment in this room. There were patients in the other rooms as well. Some groaned with pain, others were staring with vacant eyes, and most were irritable. There was a suffocating heaviness and gloom in the atmosphere. The smell of medicines, the constricting odour of chloroform and the expressionless, harsh faces of the doctors and nurses—death seemed to be lurking in every corner.

Holding some cards in one hand, the nurse went into the office on the left. The room was formidably clean; not a speck of dust. Curtains white as a shroud and a shining floor below.

The doctor was reading the complicated case history of a patient, anxiety on her face. She lifted her head to look at the nurse and returned to the case. The nurse stood by, silent. Without looking up, the doctor said, 'Yes?'

'Doctor, the patient in bed twenty-six has completed ten days today. Should she be allowed to go? We are short of beds as it is. There are several patients waiting to be admitted.'

'Has she put any money in the charity box?' the doctor asked.

'Doctor, she is very poor. She has put in only one rupee.'

'That is all right. She may be discharged.' The doctor's voice had a nasal twang. The nurse placed the card before her. She signed it, after which the nurse took the card and left.

Now she came to the free Maternity Ward and walked up to bed twenty-six. Her face wore a meaningful smile. 'You have been discharged today. Where will you go from here?'

'I don't know.' The speaker was a delicate girl of twenty-two or twenty-three. She was lively and beautiful and her figure had the pleasing, fresh fullness of budding youth. Her sari was of fine material—pale blue, with a thin border. The sleeves of her tight blouse hugged her rounded arms. Full cheeks imparted a charming innocence to her young face. Her large expressive eyes were vivacious.

'How many days have you been away from home?' asked the nurse.

'Ten months.'

'Will you remain in Delhi for some time?'

'No, I will go away tomorrow,' she said in an Urdu accent.

'Are your things in order?'

'Yes.'

Bending over her, the nurse said something in a low voice. The girl's face mirrored disappointment and defeat. She lowered her eyes. 'There is nothing to worry about, do you understand?' the nurse consoled her. The patient's nostrils were quivering.

The nurse picked up the beautiful chubby baby who lay wrapped in a green towel. His head was covered with silky curls, making him look like he wore a small black cap. The expressionless eyes of the nurse momentarily filled with love. She kissed the baby's cheek. He stirred at the nurse's touch and his lips moved, as though he were sucking milk. He was quite red, rather like raw flesh; his lips were slightly blue, as those of a newborn just beginning to suckle are apt to be. The nurse walked ahead and the girl followed behind with slow steps. She did not seem quite steady on her feet. Her face was white, as though all the blood had been drained from it. When the nurse gave her the child, her hands were like ice.

As soon as she saw the nurse, the lady who had been waiting stood up.

'Your carriage is at the back gate, isn't it?' asked the nurse.

'Yes,' replied the lady.

'That is convenient,' said the nurse. 'There is quite a crowd in front.'

The woman slipped a fat, sealed envelope into the nurse's hand and said, 'Sister, I hope you realize this is an absolutely confidential matter. You and I have known each other for years. Please keep this to yourself!'

'Thank you, madam. You can trust us completely. You are an old patient of ours. We know you very well.'

'Thank you,' came the lady's reply.

'Goodbye, then. The doctor will be starting out on her rounds soon. Please see that the gate is closed. Thank you.'

The nurse quickly went back to her office.

The carriage was standing where it had been left. The horse was sniffing the green grass, oblivious of the rest of the world. Seeing the lady approach, the driver patted the horse once more and emitted a strange noise—'Hurrr!' The horse lifted his neck and flicked off the flies from both his flanks with his short tail; his nostrils swelled as he snorted. Then he looked at the driver as though to tell him he was ready.

The lady helped the girl climb into the coach. The girl shot a subdued glance at her, then lowered her eyes. She was holding the tiny baby carelessly with one hand. She did not look at the baby even once. The lady made as if to say something to the girl but for some reason remained silent. She was staring at the child without looking away. His tiny chest rose and fell with each breath.

The driver shut the doors of the coach and climbed on top of the box. Touching the horse lightly with his whip, he said, 'Come on, son!' From a slow trot, the horse broke into a gallop.

As soon as the carriage entered, the sentry at the gate stood up stiffly and then locked the gate after the carriage had passed.

The last days of March. Winter was limping to an end, though the nights were still cold. In the long room at the end of the small courtyard, a bed was spread out with simple, rough bedding. There was a pillow without a cover. More trouble had been taken over the baby's bed. A clean white mattress and small pillows; freshly washed white diapers. The lady dressed the baby in a white kurta and a small jacket. Then she tied his diaper. The innocent little face began to look even sweeter. The mother still did not look at the child; as though it were not her child at all. She was staring fixedly at the wall. Her eyes held a mingling of fear, sadness and despair. She turned to the lady and asked, 'When do I have to go?'

'The train leaves at 5.30 in the morning.' The girl was silent. She cast a fleeting glance at the baby and her lips started quivering. She began to seek support from the wall once more. The lady looked at the child too and her heart filled with secret joy and relief, mixed in a strange way with pain. She left.

The last rays of the setting sun illuminated the wall in front. The evening was drawing to a close. Soon night covered the myriad mysteries of the world with her black mantle. There was peace now in a world of restless care. When the girl was called for dinner, she refused to eat. The lady brought her a cup of hot milk, and, after much coaxing, succeeded in making her drink it. 'What on earth will you be able to do if you're hungry?' was what she said.

She went away again. The girl did not unpack her luggage. She curled herself up in a corner of the bed. When her neck began to hurt on the hard edge of the bed, she made a pillow of her arm. Her mind turned to recollections of the past. The recent past—the closed carriage, the serious face of the lady, the forbidding sound of the horse's hooves and the thumping of her own heart. A little before that—the ten days spent in the hospital; the doctors and nurses, the smell of medicines, the groaning and sobbing patients, death, pandemonium, and then the terrifying silence. The past of ten months ago—the never-ending quarrels at home, the unbearable exchanges, discomfort, the sudden decision to leave home, the grand station of Delhi, the lady's magnificent house and then . . . .

Her wandering mind took her back seven years. She was fifteen years old then. She'd had an ostentatious wedding. Her father had sunk into debt. Hundreds of people had been invited to dinner. She was on top of the world. Her friends had looked at her with envy. The smiling, carefree face of her young husband swam before her eyes.

That carefree face . . . . Was it not her marriage to him that made her the most fortunate creature on earth? With a husband she was rich, a veritable Goddess Lakshmi. After that? The desolate grim night that same year, which had snatched away all her joys, comfort and pleasure, leaving her a long and empty life. She began to sob. Her eyes seemed to have been taken over by a flood. The tears flowed on and she did not know when she fell asleep.

It was four o'clock. The lady shook her arm gently. She started and her heart began to hammer again. The lady spoke in a low voice, 'It is four o'clock.'

'All right.'

'Will you drink some tea?'

'No.'

'Do you need anything?'

'No.'

'Is there any message?'

'No.'

'Do believe me, I won't be offended. Say anything?'

'No, nothing at all.'

'Should I come to the station with you?'

'No.'

'Should I send a servant with you?'

'No.'

The lady's heart was suddenly gripped with anguish. She went inside. The baby was still in the deep and tranquil sleep of infancy. The girl bent down and kissed the child. She caressed his soft curls. His lips again began to move as though he were sucking milk.

The lady returned. 'Will you not feed the baby one last time?'

'What time is it?'

'Five.'

'It is too late now.'

She looked at the child again and pressed her breasts with both palms. The milk had begun to flow. There was a painful lump in her throat.

'Don't worry, my dear. Your baby will be dearer to me than my own life. I do not have a child of my own and . . . this child could well have blossomed in my own womb, but . . . .' Her voice trembled, something seemed to stick in her throat and she was unable to complete the sentence. She handed the girl a thick wad of notes. 'This is to pay for your travel. All right, then. I bid you farewell.'

The girl was overcome by tenderness and gratitude. There was so much she wanted to say but her tongue failed her. She lifted a hand to her forehead in respectful greeting and climbed into the carriage. The coach rolled forward. Moist eyes were fixed on the gate.

The lady's strict hold on her emotions at last broke loose. She collapsed on the bed and her body shook with sobs. A stream of tears flowed from her eyes.

The crying of the baby roused her. Her heart began to beat loudly. Had she done the right thing, she wondered. Would she be able to shoulder this responsibility? The infant's cries gained strength. She went slowly and picked up the baby. For an instant, the features of a very dear one were reflected on the baby's face.

Should she write to Shahid abroad and tell him every thing?

It is all futile, meaningless, she thought, and a deep despair caught hold of her.

THE STEAMER
Ramkumar

Suddenly Malti felt as though the days she had held in her hands till now had flown, like a bird, far into the sky. Holding on to the railing of the steamer, she gazed at the sea that stretched into the distance.

The indolent sunlit afternoon . . . despite the commotion of people on the steamer. She sensed a deep wilderness encircling her.

'You are very quiet.' Jitu had come up and now stood beside her. Malti did not look up. Jitu knew her nature well, and, in the course of this trip to Sri Lanka, he had discovered many things about her. Though he had never really felt curious to know more about Malti.

'When I was little, I was haunted by only one dream,' Malti said, gazing at the ocean below her, 'to sit on a steamer and travel to a new land . . . the two-hour passage on this steamer today has stirred that memory again.'

Jitu laughed. He would often laugh at what Malti said.

'Why? Did you never experience such an urge?'

'I don't think of these things.'

Malti looked at him with irritation. Why did Jitu always try to laugh off whatever she said? The suppressed smile that played on Jitu's lips, even when she spoke in utmost seriousness, provoked her anger. 'Of course, you only have very lofty thoughts.'

Jitu began to quietly smoke.

'Where is Kitty?' Malti asked after a while.

Jitu was staring attentively at her. Despite her age, her face had an elusive charm and her eyes were alive with a restrained restlessness . . . . Sometimes, when alone with Malti, Jitu had been assailed by an indefinable fear. He remembered that night in Colombo when she had drunk too much whisky despite his efforts to restrain her, and had looked at him with wild eyes, as though she wanted to swallow him up. 'Jitu, maybe you'll never understand what it is like to spend your life with a man you don't love.'

She gave an unnatural laugh. 'You must have read about it in books, but, when you have to live through it, night and day, it is quite different!' With her eyes on Jitu's disturbed face, she had gone on to say many other things. Jitu had implored her to return to the hotel but without success. 'You go if you want to; I'll sit here for as long as I please. Being alone doesn't frighten me.' Her laughter had startled Jitu. 'Jitu, why do you always run away from me? Do I frighten you?' Jitu had angrily taken her hand and pulled her out of the restaurant. She sat in the taxi and wept. Jitu made no attempt to console her. That night, sitting silently in his room, he had thought about Malti for a long time.

'Do you know where Kitty is?' Malti asked again.

'She must be with Subodh. Let us go and have some tea in the restaurant.'

She leaned over the railing again. 'Is it true that it is impossible to measure the ocean? I wonder where its shore is!'

'You'll see the shore two hours later when we arrive at Dhanushkodi,' Jitu had replied in exasperation.

'If I had my way, I would spend my entire life on the sea. I have grown to despise land.' As soon as she had boarded the steamer Malti had dreaded the end of the voyage when she would have to disembark and set foot on land. Then she would be propelled forward, involuntarily, as it were, with no chance to stop anywhere in between.

They had left the coast of Sri Lanka far behind. The waves dashing wildly on the shore were visible from a distance.

'I had such an intense longing to stay on at the dak bungalow at Polonnaruwa for another two days, but none of you would listen to me. I don't think I can ever forgive you for this!' said Malti.

'You still remember that?'

'Perhaps I won't forget it as long as I live.'

Jitu felt laughter bubbling up inside him. 'Come on, we'll get ourselves some tea. I'm falling asleep.'

'You go on ahead and drink some. Kitty and Subodh are there too.'

A group of seagulls flew overhead, keeping pace with the steamer. Malti gazed at them sadly. They were plain, colourless creatures, yet their outstretched wings held a strange attraction which filled her with envy. A little later, she realized that Jitu no longer stood beside her. Perhaps he had gone into the steamer's restaurant with Kitty and Subodh. He liked Kitty's company. He would spend hours at their place. Malti quite liked being left alone. She still supported herself on the railing, but the barrier she had felt between herself and the sea was gone. The azure of the sky stretched above her and below there was as much of the sea. Standing there, she forgot about herself, so to speak. Suddenly, sensing Subodh's presence near her, she started and made an attempt to smile.

'When did you come?'

'I've been standing here for a long time,' Subodh laughed and said, 'but you were so lost in yourself . . . .'

'That is a lie!' Malti said, 'and where is Kitty?'

'She is in the restaurant with Jitu. Jitu said you wouldn't listen to him, so I came instead.'

'Jitu is still a child.'

Having known Subodh intimately for so many years, she sometimes still got the feeling that she had just met him and knew nothing about him at all. She found it difficult to believe that he was a ghost from her past that could not be resurrected. No faded image rose up in her mind when she saw Subodh and Kitty in the role of husband and wife, though, for some reason, just momentarily, she perceived their relationship to be very superficial. Subodh bent over the railing too. The strong breeze was playing havoc with his already tangled hair. Subodh was such an old friend of hers! Even after he married Kitty, a thread of their relationship had remained unbroken.

'I am quite fed up with this journey. I want to get home as quickly as possible,' said Subodh.

At the mention of 'home', Malti's hand trembled. Whenever the thought of home occurred to her, she quickly tried to push it away. At least for the duration of this trip, she wanted to forget those little knots which had become so inextricably tied to her life.

'Do you know, Subodh, the first question I asked the palmist when I was a child concerned the length of my travel line!' Malti said. Subodh laughed. He was looking at Malti intently.

A tremor went through Malti and she looked down.

'This is the last day of our journey,' she found herself saying.

'There are two days left, yet.'

'They will be spent on the train,' said Malti softly. 'Subodh, I wanted to ask you something. Was Kitty upset the other day because you were taking a walk with me?'

Subodh tried to laugh, which convinced Malti that he would never tell her the truth. 'This is a futile discussion,' he said.

Malti did not hear what he said. She was finding it difficult to control her tears. She turned her face away so that Subodh could not see her. 'Let's go into the restaurant and have some tea. Kitty and Jitu must be waiting for us,' said Subodh.

The restaurant resounded with the hubbub of travellers. A transistor was pouring out music. As soon as Malti sat down, a feeling of extreme weariness caught up with her. She glanced at Kitty momentarily. Kitty had done her hair, applied a dash of make-up and changed her sari after she had boarded the steamer. Malti always felt a little inadequate in Kitty's presence. Kitty was no longer young; strands of silver gleamed in her dark hair, yet there was an inherent attractiveness in her personality, which Malti, indefinably, found lacking in herself.

'Malti doesn't want to get off the steamer,' said Jitu. 'We should get her a ticket on a steamer that is going round the world!'

Kitty smiled and looked at Malti. 'The very idea of travelling on a steamer makes me giddy!'

'Malti was just saying that she hates land,' Jitu said.

Malti felt an upsurge of resentment, 'Why do you always speak on my behalf, Jitu?'

Kitty began to pour the tea out. Malti did not object to people talking about her. In fact, it made her feel more important than Kitty. She had often tried to convince herself that in many ways she was better off than Kitty—she had friends of her own; a life in which her husband never interfered; no dearth of money. Yet, when it got to Subodh, the argument came to a standstill . . . .

Late into that night, at the dak bungalow in Anuradhapura, she had thought of so many things. Subodh, Kitty, Jitu—there were times when she had considered the idea of leaving them at the dak bungalow and going off into the darkness of the night. This idea was not new to her. Earlier, too, looking at her husband asleep on the bed, she had been seized with an impulse to leave the house silently; no one would even know. Yet, she was not herself sure what bonds kept her firmly in their grip.

A football team travelling from Sri Lanka to India was in the restaurant too. A rowdy bunch of youths . . . laughing, full of enthusiasm, dressed in their playing clothes! A wave of eagerness had swept over her.

'Tell me, Jitu, have you ever played football?' asked Malti suddenly.

Subodh burst out laughing. Kitty smiled and looked at Malti.

They could see only the heads of people walking on the deck. Malti looked at Subodh's watch, and it occurred to her that only an hour remained of the voyage. She could not bring herself to talk about this to anyone.

'What are you thinking about, Malti?' asked Kitty suddenly, in a subdued voice.

Malti smiled. Kitty's sympathy always annoyed her. She stood up, all at once. 'It is suffocating in here. I'm going up to the deck.' She left her tea unfinished.

'Malti is bored of the same people,' she heard Jitu say, but she proceeded to the door without a word.

There was not a soul about at the opposite end of the steamer. Because that section of the steamer did not have a roof, the sun beat down mercilessly, but the powerful wind sheltered Malti from the heat. She could see a flock of seagulls before her.

Bent over the railing, the memory of many moments in Sri Lanka swam past her. Kandy, Galle, Polonnaruwa, the ruins at Anuradhapura, the tea gardens, Mount Lavinia Hotel . . . she had quite a collection of memories! Watching the waves of the deep blue ocean breaking on the shore at Galle, they had sat down there for a short while. She had smiled to herself when she saw Subodh in swimming trunks. Kitty had refused to bathe. She had tucked up her sari and strolled along the edge of the water. Malti had not done even that. She had just sat on the sand, lost in thought. For the first time on that trip she had felt like an onlooker, nothing more.

Two youths stood talking a little away from her. Maybe they were players from the football team.

Subodh and Kitty had gone out alone that day in Colombo. She had been left with Jitu. They had waited for them but it was midnight before the couple returned. She did not eat from sheer vexation, nor did she speak to Jitu. A little later she went to her room and lay down on the bed. Afterwards, she felt a pang of regret at her own foolishness.

Malti opened her purse and took out the letter Nikunj had written to her. She looked at it for some time without opening it, but it seemed to be a useless scrap of paper which had no meaning. Familiarity, leading to intimacy that lasted a few days . . . then nothing at all; as though it had never happened. Subodh and Jitu had poked fun at Nikunj. 'You are driving poor Nikunj round the bend, Malti!' Subodh had said. 'He will commit suicide when you leave,' said Jitu. She had kept laughing.

Subodh knows every thing, Malti thought. Perhaps he knew even more about her than she did herself, yet he pretended ignorance. Many times she had taken the decision to break off all ties with Subodh; she made up her mind never to see him again, yet, whenever she saw him, she could not restrain herself.

Malti held on tight to the railing; she felt as though somebody were pushing her into the sea from behind. Before her, the sun's rays glanced off the calm sea, making it glint like a sheet of silver.

The idea had occurred to her that perhaps she could stay on in Sri Lanka for a few more days by herself. Subodh had work at the office, Kitty was eager to see her children, Jitu had to study, but she nothing to do and no desire to return. She could have been with Nikunj and coped with her loneliness in this way. Her husband would have created no problems. However, the idea of abandoning Subodh, Kitty and Jitu had burdened her with the guilt of betrayal. Perhaps it was simply the attraction Subodh exercised on her that compelled her forward relentlessly. Looking at Subodh sitting opposite her in the train, on the very first day of their journey, she had thought to herself that here Subodh would not be in a hurry to get home and she would be able to see him for the whole day. This prospect had thrilled her into laughter.

She clung to the frail railing that she could so easily have gone over. Yet she found she could not break away from the ties that held her captive even when freedom was within reach. How, then, could she blame others?

Suddenly she started, seeing the two youths standing next to her.

'Did you tour around Sri Lanka?' one of them asked.

She nodded.

'To which places did you go?'

'Kandy, Galle, Anuradhapura and many other places.'

'We are going to India for the first time. Where do you live?'

For a split second she could not remember the name of the town.

'We are going to play football. Are you interested in football?'

She began to laugh. 'I was, once, but now it is ages since I saw a match.'

They invited her to see the match. They were students of Kandy University. They had healthy bodies and lively eyes. The prospect of seeing a new place made their faces shine with excitement. Malti sensed a host of forgotten things stirring to life within her.

When they had left, Malti became aware that she still held Nikunj's letter in her hand. This was the letter Nikunj had written to her three or four days back. She felt no desire to open and read it. She tore it up and threw it into the sea. For some time she could see the small bits of white paper swimming in the sea. Emptiness echoed inside her.

At times she felt she was losing the strength to keep up the struggle. She had a suspicion that her husband, Subodh and Kitty all felt that soon she would let herself go, just like those bits of paper that floated along with the current. This thought filled her with a loathing for herself.

From a distance she could see Jitu, Subodh and Kitty heading in her direction. They were in deep conversation. She felt an intense fury sweep over her. She had nothing in common with them, they would never be able to understand her with her inner struggles and complexes . . . .

'What are you doing here alone, Malti?' asked Jitu. Standing there alone, she had startled them. Subodh looked at her seriously. Malti was afraid of this look. It seemed to want to gather all of her up.

'Malti has chosen the best spot on the deck,' said Kitty. 'Standing here we can't even tell we are on a steamer. We seem to be flying above the sea.'

The wind blew their hair back. Jitu smoked a cigarette; Subodh had his hands in his pockets and watched the sea. 'If we had halted for some time at Dhanushkodi, we could have seen Rameshwaram,' said Jitu.

'I won't stop anywhere now. I am so tired of seeing places that I only want to stop where there is nothing at all to see,' said Kitty.

'You are missing your children, Kitty,' Jitu said with a laugh.

'Yes, and why not? This is the first time I have left them alone for so long,' said Kitty. 'Tell me, Subodh, are you sure there is no train from Madras at night? We do have to spend the night there?'

'Well, you can ask them yourself this time, since you don't believe me,' Subodh peevishly replied.

The tension on Malti's face lessened by degrees. She felt herself at a great distance from the others.

'Malti is missing the dak bungalow at Polonnaruwa,' Kitty said, looking at Malti.

'That dak bungalow really was very beautiful. The sound of the lake beating softly against the wall was very musical . . . .'

'Such places frighten me. I could not sleep that night,' Kitty said.

Jitu had a vague feeling that Malti was angry. He began to laugh. On this voyage, Kitty, Subodh, Malti, all had seemed to him to be characters from an intriguing novel, and he had been unable to reach a definite conclusion about any of them. Whenever he did form an opinion, some small incident forced him to revise it. He was not involved with anybody else; he was just an onlooker.

'Why did you laugh, Jitu?' Kitty asked.

'Why did you suddenly grow so serious the other evening? You were too vexed to even speak!' As soon as he spoke, he realized this was not a question he should have asked in public. Who was he to interfere in the affairs of others?

Kitty blushed and tried to smile.

'You are yet a child, Jitu,' said Subodh, after a momentary silence. 'You know very little about women, especially middle-aged women.'

Malti suppressed her laughter with difficulty. Jitu was amused too. 'Middle-aged . . . .' He looked towards Subodh. 'Kitty and Malti can't be called middle-aged.'

'What about middle-aged men?' asked Kitty. 'Do you suppose they are easy to understand?'

'Anybody who doesn't know Subodh would think he is a university student!' said Jitu.

Subodh tried to laugh off his embarrassment. Jitu is right, thought Malti. There had hardly been any change in Subodh in fifteen years. Not one grey hair and not a wrinkle on his face! The same sparkle in his eyes and that child-like laughter . . . maybe he would never grow middle-aged. She liked this thought.

'Listen, Malti,' Kitty said, 'do you remember the time when Subodh would spend the entire day sitting in the canteen? Don't you think there is a world of a difference between then and now? Jitu didn't know him then!'

Malti, however, did not want to remember those days. Whenever she was alone and did remember, she wanted to forget them at once.

A patch of cloud drifted just above their heads.

Subodh looked at his watch. 'Another half an hour to go. I'm bored of being on this deck!'

'I am very tired,' Kitty said.

There was only half an hour left—the very thought was frightening to Malti. After a three-hour halt at Dhanushkodi, the same steamer would return to Sri Lanka, but with different passengers. She tucked her unruly hair back into her bun.

Jitu and Subodh went over to the other side of the deck to look after the luggage. Malti had once been very close to Kitty, but now she found an ever-present dim shadow lurking between them. There were so many topics on which they could never openly speak. When they were left alone, they would indulge only in small talk.

'I just met two boys from the football team. They said we must go to see their match,' said Malti.

Kitty did not hear what she said. There were times when deep and mysterious shadows played across Kitty's face and then Malti would find it impossible to catch a glimpse of what went on inside her. Her children, her home, her children . . . that was as far as she could see.

'A single seagull is an ugly creature, yet in a crowd its ugliness seems to get dispersed,' said Kitty seriously.

'A seagull symbolizes a journey. Whenever I see one, I feel I am about to travel,' said Malti, looking at the gulls. Kitty was silent. 'Do you know, for the past few months I have been dreaming constantly about travelling? Maybe I am really preparing to go on a long journey.'

At the other end of the deck, the clamour of the passengers was progressively increasing. Because of the noise made by the wind, the din seemed to come from a long way off.

'Come, I think we are arriving at Dhanushkodi,' Kitty said.

Malti followed her even though she had no desire to do so. The passengers were piling up their luggage near the door. The players of the football team were engrossed in talking to each other. Malti cast an indifferent gaze on every one. A deep dejection enveloped her. She became aware that her head was throbbing slightly. She had the feeling she had traversed many difficult paths in the two hours spent on the steamer.

On the shore, dim outlines could be seen. Gradually, they transformed themselves into familiar shapes—trees, houses, the shore . . . .

'There is the land!' said Jitu triumphantly. Everyone was looking in the same direction. Each passenger on board was in a hurry to get off the steamer. Malti grasped the railing tightly. She was afraid that if she stood without support, she might fall.

'Subodh, you go on ahead and reserve four berths,' said Kitty. 'If we can't get a place to sleep, we'll be in trouble.'

Kitty had repeated this several times. They were all familiar with this little habit of hers. It irked Subodh.

The sleepy afternoon sun . . . Malti stood silently by the railing. A few locks of hair had escaped on to her forehead. So many paths had beckoned to her in her search for a direction, yet they always brought her back to her own doorstep. She felt that after all these years, she should make her truce with this fact. Yet she continued to make the same mistake and felt piqued at herself when she remembered.

They had come up close to the shore now. The sound of the steamer hooting sent a shiver through Malti's body.

'I'm just coming,' she said as she went into the toilet. She locked it from the inside and stood quietly for a while. She had an impulse to cry, yet her being rebelled against such an easy acceptance of defeat. She washed her face and applied cream and powder onto it; then she combed her hair and put on the perfume she had bought in Colombo, the one Subodh had appreciated several times.

When she emerged from the toilet, the steamer was stationary. A crowd of people, railway carriages and soldiers could be seen on the shore. Beyond them, Malti could see the flat, lonely road that stretched ahead for miles and which would end when it reached her house.

MARRIED WOMEN
Mohan Rakesh

Manorama got a start when she entered the room. Kashi stood in front of the dressing-table, Manorama's sari draped over her head. Lipstick coloured her lips, and, her face, plastered with powder, looked sinister. Oblivious to this, however, she gazed with rapt attention at her reflection in the mirror. A storm of anger swept over Manorama as soon as she saw her.

'Kashi *Mai*!' she shouted loudly, 'whatever are you doing?'

Hurriedly removing the sari from her head, Kashi jumped away from the dressing-table. Terrified at Manorama's anger, she broke into a sheepish grin as she became aware of the impersonation she had been caught out on.

'*Didi*! I beg you to forgive me!' she entreated. 'I was tidying up the room and when I came to the mirror I couldn't help myself! You can subtract the damages from my wages if you like!'

'Your wages!' Kashi's words only fanned Manorama's anger. 'You get a wage of fifteen rupees and you expect me to deduct six-and-a-half from it for lipstick? You break dishes, steal ghee, sugar and flour all the time but I turn a blind eye to every thing. The other servants complain that you don't do a spot of work and are disobedient to boot. The committee members are after me to fire you because they are sick of listening to your tale of woe. I keep you on, nevertheless, and this is the way you pay me back! You ungrateful wretch!'

She pulled up a cane chair roughly, as though it were guilty of an offence, and, sitting down, she passed a cold hand over her forehead. Kashi was silent.

'She's getting on to forty but still nurses a desire to doll up,' Manorama grumbled again. 'The slut!'

Throwing her head back, she closed her eyes. The day at school had drained her mind and her body was tired too. She had just been to the public library and then taken a long walk hoping it would cheer her up, but a strange despondency had settled on her as she made her way back. The sun had set when she was about half a mile from her house. Then the mantle of gloom had lifted itself. The wind rustling through the trees, stirring each leaf, and the clouds sailing across the sky, had touched her with intoxication. The pale evening moonlight was slowly acquiring colour. Tucking back the end of her sari she took a few brisk steps.

By the time she reached the corner, however, her enthusiasm vanished, and, when she reached the school gate, she did not even want to go in. But she forced herself to push the gate open. It wouldn't do for the headmistress of the Girls' High School to roam the streets alone at night. When, against her will, she climbed the steps to her quarters, this spectacle had met her eyes.

She opened her eyes and her anger mounted when she saw Kashi still standing there, as though she had hoped Kashi would disappear when she shut her eyes.

'What's the point in hanging around here now?' she snapped. 'Go away!'

Kashi's face registered no special effect of the rebuke. In fact, she approached closer and sat down on the floor.

'*Didi*, I beg you to forgive me!' she implored, catching hold of Manorama's feet. Manorama wrested her feet away and got up abruptly.

'I told you to leave me alone! Stop bothering me!' She walked to the window as she spoke. Kashi stood up too.

'Shall I make some tea for you? You must be tired after that walk.'

'Just go away. I don't want any tea.'

'In that case, I'll get you some food.'

Manorama silently looked away.

'*Didi* I entreat you to pardon me!'

Manorama said nothing, though she pressed a hand to her head.

'I'll press your head if you've got a headache,' offered Kashi, wiping her hands with her sari.

'I've told you to go away; why are you carrying on like this?' shouted Manorama.

Kashi fell back as though wounded. She gazed at Manorama, struck speechless for a minute. Then she went out on to the veranda. She turned around, as though to say something, then decided against it. Manorama stood at the window for as long as

Kashi's footsteps sounded on the wooden staircase. Then she lay down on the bed, a hand pressed to her forehead.

She blamed herself entirely. Any other headmistress would have turned out this woman long ago. She took more advantage of Manorama just because she was lenient with her. What nonsense she put up with, from the woman's children as well! They made a din on her stairs the whole day and dirtied the school compound too. Once she had bought them some candy. After that they clung to her sari whenever they saw her, demanding candy. How she wished they'd stay clean! She had even stitched knickers for the older girl, Kunti. It had made no difference, though. The girls stayed dirty as usual, and continued to fool around. On the last inspection day they had scribbled with coal all over the schoolroom floor and she'd had to get the place cleaned again. They would often poke out their tongue at guests too. She was the only one who could tolerate all this.

She stared up at the ceiling for a while, then went out onto the veranda. The sound of her own footsteps on the wooden veranda sent shivers running down her body. She placed a hand on the pillar.

Moonlight streamed into the compound. The lines of cement made a complicated criss-cross on the brick floor. Desks, stools and blackboards lay in the school veranda creating the illusion that sinister spirits peered from their dens. The dense deodar jungle seemed to quiver at the cold touch of moonlight. It was quite deserted. Kashi's quarter had never seemed so quiet at this time. Usually her children created a commotion till nine or ten at night.

At this time one would have thought the quarter uninhabited. Because the skylights had been jammed up with cardboard, it was impossible to tell whether a lantern burned inside. Manorama gripped the pillar tighter, as though it were her only kin and she wanted to remind it of her presence. The sighing of the wind in the clump of deodars came closer and then died away in the distance.

'Kunti!' Manorama called out.

The wind carried her voice far away. The rustling forest had come very close to her again. Kashi's door opened and Kunti stood there, looking strange, as though she were shrinking into herself. Manorama motioned to her to come upstairs. Kunti looked back once and then went upstairs, cautiously.

'What's your mother doing?' Manorama tried to keep her voice from sounding dry.

'Nothing at all,' said Kunti with a vague movement of her head.

'Surely there is something that she is doing . . . .'

'She is weeping.'

'Why, what's she crying for?'

Kunti preferred not to reply. Manorama silently looked down. 'Haven't you eaten yet?' she asked after a momentary pause.

'Father is arriving tonight. Mother says we'll eat together.'

Every thing was as clear as daylight to Manorama now. Kashi had told her that Ajudhya was coming back after an absence of three years. No wonder Kashi had felt like dolling up today. Maybe that was the reason why her children were so quiet too. Their father was coming home . . . the father they had not seen for three years, and one whom they probably would not recognize. Or maybe they would—as a stern stentorian voice and a heavy hand that delivered blows . . . .

'Go and send your mother upstairs,' she said gently, patting Kunti's shoulder. 'Tell her I'd like to see her.'

Kunti went downstairs, her shoulders and arms again giving the odd impression that they were shrinking. Kashi appeared a little later. She had obviously been crying. Her eyes were red and she kept wiping her nose with her sari.

'Are you crying just because I scolded you a little?' asked Manorama as soon as she saw her.

'That's how it is with masters and servants, *Didi*!'

'You dissolve into tears just because you're ticked off for doing something wrong!' Manorama tried to join something broken. 'Go and wash your face in the bathroom.'

Kashi, however, just stood there, wiping her eyes and nose. Manorama rubbed her hands together nervously. 'Is Ajudhya arriving today?' she queried. Kashi inclined her head.

'Is he going to stay for some time or will he leave immediately?'

'All he's written is that he'll leave once he has given the apple trees out on rent.'

Manorama was aware that Ajudhya had some family property and the apple trees on it were let out on contract every year. Kashi had let out the trees last year for a hundred-and-twenty-five and for a hundred-and-fifty the year before. Ajudhya had written her a very harsh letter last year implying that Kashi took extra money from the contractors which she was keeping for herself. Kashi wrote to him saying that he should himself undertake the negotiations this time; she was in no mood to entertain accusations in money matters. Ajudhya had abandoned her five years ago to live with another woman in Pathankot. He had set up a grocery shop there, but never sent Kashi any money.

'Is he coming all the way from Pathankot just to collect the rent?' asked Manorama, though her mind was obviously elsewhere. 'He'll spend half the money on the fare.'

'I thought he might stay this time at least for the children's sake!' Emotion tinged Kashi's voice. 'Besides, he can find out for himself that no one pays a hundred-and-fifty for these apples now.'

'Why, what a weird fellow!' Manorama's voice held a note of sympathy. 'What if you do keep away some money? After all, you're rearing the children. He should send you some money every month . . . instead, he talks like this?'

'*Didi*, who can win a man over!' Kashi's voice became even more pathetic.

'Then why don't you tell him that . . . .' Manorama checked herself in mid-sentence. She remembered that a few days ago she had resented similar questions from Kashi when she'd got a letter from Sushil. There were many things Kashi had wanted to know . . . that if Babuji earned so much himself, why did he expect her to work? And why didn't they have any children yet? Did she keep her salary to herself or did she send some of it to Babuji?

At that moment she had laughed off Kashi's questions but deep within her she realized that Kashi had touched a sensitive chord and this knowledge had saddened her for many days.

'Shall I get your dinner?' asked Kashi, composing her voice a little.

'No, I'm not hungry yet,' said Manorama, very gently in order to assure Kashi that she was no longer angry. 'When I'm hungry, I'll help myself. You go on and finish your work. Ajudhya will be here any minute. The last bus gets in at nine.'

Manorama stood there, resting against the pillar, after Kashi left. The wind had gained strength. She felt restless. She remembered the long walks in the hills with Sushil soon after they were married. All else in the world had seemed meaningless compared to their romance. She shivered each time Sushil held her hand. The rustling forest danced inside her. When Sushil moved away, she clung to him, revelling in the thought that a tiny being was taking shape within her. This was a constant source of wonder; could a living, moving thing actually acquire form within her? She wanted to experience this miracle, she had often confided to Sushil.

However, he did not want a child around the house for some time yet. To begin with, it would ruin her figure and then it would put her job in jeopardy. Sushil was not in favour of her quitting her job to become a humdrum housewife. Besides, he had to arrange for his sister's, Ummi's, wedding in a few months and he also had two younger brothers in college. Each paisa was precious. This was why he wanted to economize at least for four or five years.

She had been unable to satisfy her desire for a child, yet an unknown child struggled to come into her arms whenever Sushil caressed her. She seemed to hear its childish peals of laughter and feel the touch of its tender body. In such moments, Sushil's face looked like a child's and she hugged him close to her. She longed to soothe him with lullabies.

It was many days since she had last got Sushil's letter. She was unbearably lonely when he didn't reply promptly, she'd told him. She had contemplated writing to him again, but her pride stood in the way. Didn't Sushil have the time to scribble even a few lines to her?

There was a strong gust of breeze. The rustling of the deodar trees was lost in the distant sky. Two circles of light were crawling forward from the direction of the hill in front. It was probably the last bus from Pathankot. The thick slats of the gate glinted in the moonlight. The wind pushed against the gate, as though it wanted to break open the lock. Manorama took a deep breath and returned inside. She felt intensely lonely today.

Back from her walk the next evening, Manorama stopped at the gate, startled. She could hear a loud noise from Kashi's quarter. Ajudhya was obviously thrashing her, cursing loudly all the while. Kashi wailed at the top of her voice. Manorama shook with rage. According to the committee rules, no male could enter the school at night. It was only due to the special allowance she'd made for him that Ajudhya had been able to stay there. And look at the audacity of the man! What bothered Manorama was not the beating that Kashi was being subjected to but the fact that such an incident would give a bad reputation to the school, which in turn would reflect on the headmistress . . . .

She climbed up the stairs to her quarters quickly. Tap-tap-tap—her sandals resounded on the wooden staircase. She was not quite sure what she should do. Would it be better to call Kashi and tell her to send Ajudhya packing at once, or should she summon Ajudhya himself and let him know that he must leave by morning?

As soon as entered the veranda, the first person she saw was Kunti, who sat in a corner, a hangdog look on her face, as though she felt the pain from the blows landing on her mother. Manorama was nonplussed at the sight of the girl sitting there at this time. 'What's the matter?' she asked, keeping her anger in check.

'*Amma* asked me to serve your dinner . . . .' She looked at Manorama apprehensively, as though she expected her to grab her by the arm right away and start beating her.

'Can you get my dinner?'

Kunti nodded in the same frightened manner.

'What's that commotion in your quarter?' Manorama's tone implied that she held Kunti responsible for what was happening there. Kunti's lips trembled and tears started to her eyes.

'What's he thrashing your mother for?' Manorama repeated her question.

Kunti wiped her eyes with her shirt, holding back her tears. She said, 'He took out all the money from *Amma*'s box and when she tried to restrain him he started beating her.'

'This man is a lunatic!' Sparks of anger flared up in Manorama. 'He'll come to his senses when I throw him out of here!'

Kunti continued to sob and then spoke: 'He accused *Amma* of keeping part of the rent for herself. This time he's let out the trees for two hundred. *Amma* had sixty or seventy rupees. He's taken them all.'

There was something so pathetic in Kunti's expression that Manorama hugged her close without bothering about her dirty clothes.

'Don't cry,' she said, caressing her. 'I'll get your mother's money back from him. You carry on inside.'

Manorama washed Kunti's face in the kitchen herself and then sat down on a care stool. She began to chew silently on the roti that Kunti had put in her plate. She would not have put up with such food had Kashi cooked it. Some of the chapatis were undercooked while the others were half-burnt, and all looked different. The grains of dal were still hard. However, she broke off bits of chapati mechanically and swallowed them after dipping them in the dal, rather in the manner in which she signed papers at the office every day, or attended to the grievances of the teachers. Kunti gave her a start when she placed another chapati in her plate without asking her.

'No, I don't want any more,' she said, moving her hand forward, as if the chapati had not reached her plate yet. She began to break little bits from it distractedly. The noise below had ceased. Soon she heard the sound of the gate being opened and then shut. She guessed Ajudhya must be going out. She said to Kunti, who was shutting the container of chapatis, 'Go tell your mother to lock the gate as usual. It shouldn't be open at night.'

Kunti nodded silently and went on with her work.

'Tell her to come upstairs later, too.'

Her voice had acquired a note of severity again. Kunti gazed at her, as though she were a particularly difficult lesson in her book that she had failed to comprehend even after utmost effort. Then she shook her head and went back to work.

Kashi sat with Manorama late into the night. What Kashi held against Ajudhya was not the thrashing he'd given her but his lack of interest in the children even after three long years. Perhaps his mistress had acquired occult power from a saint, which kept him in her hold, for he always did what she told him to. The astrologer she'd been to see said that the spell could not be broken for seven years. He also told Kashi, though, that one day his illegitimate children would eat her children's leftovers, wear clothes discarded by them. She was waiting for that day.

Manorama listened to her but nothing registered. She kept wondering why Sushil had not written . . . it was getting to be a month since she wrote but he had not bothered to reply. A lock of hair had strayed on to her forehead. Its soft touch sent little tremors through her body. She forgot momentarily that Kashi sat there talking to her. Each time the tendril of hair on her forehead stirred she felt she caressed the tender skin of a baby. Days flashed upon her memory, days when Sushil's fingers had played with her hair and his lips had bent over each pulsating part of her body . . . .

It was odd that Sushil had taken so long to write back. There were many letters in the post for her every day, but they were all addressed to the headmistress. It was days since there had been a letter for Manorama Sachdeva . . . . When she had come back after the vacation this time, she had promised to send warm fabric for

Sushil's coat as soon as possible. And a shawl for Ummi too. Was Sushil annoyed that she had not kept her promise?

Kashi made as if to leave and Manorama again became aware of the loneliness encircling her. The murmuring deodar forest, moonlight glimmering on the River Ravi in the distant valley and her own sleepy eyes . . . perhaps there was an invisible link between them. Kashi had reached the veranda when she called her back, asking her to lock the gate properly before she went to bed and to send Kunti in to her; she would like the girl to sleep in her house tonight.

She kept awake late into the night. The clean, sparkling sky, visible from her windows, stretched into the distance. Passing gusts of breeze set the rows of pine and deodar dancing, assuming myriad postures. The sighing of the wind slipping off the branches so exhilarated her that she felt a sort of numb rapture stealing over her. She sat for some time, her head resting on the window-sill. When she closed her eyes for a minute, she imagined that her head was resting against Sushil's chest. The wind, she imagined, was carrying her away, far away . . . beyond the pine and deodar forest, across the glistening water of the Ravi . . . .

She moved away from the window to lie down. A square of moonlight, streaming in from the skylight, illuminated the face of Kunti asleep on the other bed. Manorama got a start. She had never thought Kunti so beautiful before. Her lips were shapely and tender, half-open, like the new red leaves of a mango tree. Manorama leaned over the bed on her elbows to get a closer look. Then, with an abrupt movement, she kissed her. Kunti stirred in her sleep.

Manorama rested against the pillow, gazing at the ceiling. Overcome by sleep, she started at the sound of the gate opening and then closing. Soon after that, Ajudhya could again be heard grumbling in Kashi's quarter. He sounded drunk. A wave of anger came over Manorama again. She wrapped herself tightly in the blanket and tried to forget that voice, but it haunted her even when she was asleep.

Ajudhya left after two days and Manorama heaved a sigh of relief. She had constantly dreaded that she would lose control of herself any moment and ask the peon to push the man out of the school grounds. A look at the man's face was enough to betray how mean he was. His large and dirty teeth, dark lips and piercing eyes, resembling a ferocious animal, made one feel that the man should be given a life sentence. She felt considerably lighter once he had left. She managed to complete many trivial tasks at the office which she had been putting off for days. That same evening she got Sushil's letter too.

She did not open the letter at the office. She decided to dictate the rest of her letters to the stenographer the following day and went back to her quarters. She made herself comfortable on the bed and slit the envelope open very slowly with a paper knife, as though she feared to hurt it. The letter had been hurriedly scrawled on office paper. Manorama didn't like that, but, nevertheless, read each line eagerly.

Sushil wrote that Ummi's engagement would soon be finalized. The boy had a lucrative job and everybody had approved of the match. Could she possibly send Ummi's shawl soon? Now they should save up for Ummi's wedding as well. At the end of it all, he asked her to take care of herself. He concluded with sweet embraces and countless kisses.

Manorama sat holding the letter for a long time. She had read it many times over, but those loving embraces and hundreds of kisses did not come across to her at all. It was as though she had bent over to drink from a cool spring but her lips had brushed against wet sand instead. She put the letter away in a drawer and returned to the office.

Through with dinner that night, she sat down intending to reply to the letter. However, as soon as she picked up the pen, her mind seemed to go blank. She felt she had nothing to say at all. After the first line, she sat there scratching the paper with her nail. After much effort, she wrote a few more lines. When she read the letter again, she thought it wasn't very different from the ones she dictated to the clerk at the office. The only relevant point she had made was that she was sorry for not having sent the shawl and the material for the coat yet. She would do it soon now. She ended off with sweet embraces, and countless kisses too . . . .

Late into the night she tried to come to a decision as to what expenditure she could cut down on so as to save an extra forty or fifty rupees every month. Should she give up drinking milk? Wash her own clothes? Or maybe she should fire Kashi and cook for herself? Kashi was largely responsible for her mounting expenses. Not only did she demand things from Manorama, she stole as well.

Yet this was an experiment that had failed earlier when she had tried it. She could not cook when she came back from school. She either satisfied herself with bread and milk, or she hurriedly fried something just to quieten the pangs of hunger.

She started to stint on her food the next day. She instructed Kashi that she was to get milk only sufficient for tea and to use the minimum amount of ghee for dal and vegetables. She went without biscuits and fruit. A few days flew past in the enthusiasm of saving. Then the effect of the rationing began to tell on her health. Twice she had dizzy spells while teaching, but she did not abandon her whim. She kept forty rupees aside for the shawl from that month's salary. While putting the money away, she imagined that Sushil stood before her and the expression on her face seemed to taunt him. See, this is what saving for a shawl and coat involves! Anyway, a certain peevishness had become part of her nature; she snapped at every body for nothing at all.

She startled herself when she stood before the mirror one day. The pallor of her face at once struck her. She developed a severe headache at the office and returned to her rooms even before noon. She noticed that Kashi shut the cupboard quickly and went to the stove as soon as she heard her footsteps. She walked into the kitchen and flung the cupboard open.

The tin of ghee was open and had fresh finger marks. Manorama glanced at Kashi. Ghee was smeared on her face too and she was trying to wipe her fingers surreptitiously on her sari. Manorama was furious. Coming up close to her, she grabbed her by the plait. 'You thief!' she yelled. 'Aren't you ashamed of yourself, swallowing the ghee while I eat dried-up vegetables, you despicable creature? Get out of here at once! I don't want to see you again!' She delivered a kick onto Kashi's back so that the woman almost fell over, but Kashi somehow managed to support herself on her hands. Her eyes shut for a minute in pain. Then she grabbed hold of Manorama's feet, at a complete loss for words.

'I'm giving you twenty-four hours notice,' said Manorama, extricating her feet. 'You'd better vacate the school quarter by this time tomorrow. The clerk will settle your account in the morning. After that, if you're seen in this compound, then . . . .' She started to go away but Kashi moved forward and grasped her feet again.

'*Didi*, I beg you most humbly to forgive me!' she blurted out after much effort. Manorama jerked her feet away again. One foot hit against the teapot which smashed. For an instant the sound of splintering glass stunned them both. Then, biting into her lower lip, Manorama rushed out of the kitchen. She rubbed some balm into her forehead when she reached her room, and, covering her face and head, lay down.

There was another letter from Sushil in the evening post. Its contents were more or less the same. Ummi had got engaged. They had been on a picnic with her fiance on Sunday last. Ummi, too, had scribbled a few lines in a corner, reiterating her request for the shawl. She also said that everyone missed Manorama at the picnic.

She went for a long walk once she had finished reading the letter. A feeling of extreme annoyance was building up in her. She could not quite work out who she was angry with—Kashi, Sushil or herself? For some reason there seemed to be many more pebbles on the road than there used to be and the circular road seemed much longer than she remembered it. She had to sit down twice from sheer exhaustion. Her sandals broke when she was just a few furlongs away from home. She traversed the distance with much difficulty, with the dismal feeling that she had been dragging herself along that road for days and that she had no idea how far she had yet to go . . . .

When she reached the gate the incident of the morning came to her afresh. Kashi's quarter was silent once more. She had a fleeting thought that Kashi had already left and she was all by herself in that huge compound. A tremor shot through her. She called out to Kunti who emerged from her quarter, lantern in hand.

'Where's your mother?' Manorama queried.

'She's inside,' said Kunti, glancing into the room once.

'What is she doing there?'

'Nothing much. She's just sitting there.'

Manorama noticed that Kashi's quarter was in bad shape. The frame supporting the door was worn out. The door was falling apart. She passed that way several times every day but had never noticed the state the door was in. 'This place badly needs repair,' she remarked and walked in as though to inspect it. Kashi rose and approached her. Manorama shot a look at her but preferred to say nothing. The walls of the quarter, already pale, were now acquiring a blackish hue. A skylight had detached itself from the wall and looked as though it would crash any minute. Cobwebs under the eaves had intertwined to form a sort of canopy. The few things in the room were scattered about carelessly. Three grimy children sat on one side eating chapatis from a single plate; the watery dal was similar to the one Kunti had cooked for her that day when every dried-up chapati had been a different shape . . . .

The children stopped eating when they saw her. The youngest boy, about four years old, lay wrapped up in a quilt in a corner. His eyes followed Manorama about the room.

'What's wrong with Parsu? Is he sick?' asked Manorama, looking away from Kashi as though she wanted the information from the wall. She went over to the child. Parsu fixed his eyes on his toe.

'He's got rickets,' Kashi said softly.

Manorama stroked the child's cheek and brushed a hand over his hair. 'Have you consulted a doctor?'

'Yes, I did,' said Kashi, 'he's prescribed ten injections; each one costs two rupees.' Kashi was choking on her words.

'Well, haven't you had him injected?'

Kashi's eyes were riveted to the floor. 'He took all the money I had . . . . I rub him regularly with a bell-metal bowl. They say that's a cure.'

The child stared at them with beady eyes. Stroking his cheek once more, Manorama walked to the door. Kashi stood at the threshold; she stepped aside to let Manorama pass.

'This quarter should be whitewashed,' said Manorama, on her way out. 'The place is enough to make a healthy person sick!'

She slowly made her way back to her own rooms. Tap-tapping footsteps, the lonely veranda, her room. She noticed that the mess she had left in the room had been sorted out, the scattered things now arranged neatly. The tray of chapatis had been covered and placed in the middle of the table. The kettle was singing on the stove. When she took off her coat to drape her shawl around her, she heard footsteps on the veranda. Kashi appeared and stood silently near the door.

'What is it?' Manorama asked drily.

'I've come to serve dinner.' Kashi's voice was slow, controlled. 'The water's boiling. If you like I can make you some tea first.'

Manorama glanced at her once and then looked away. Kashi entered the room and got the kettle going again. In the meantime Manorama had settled down with a book. Soon Kashi brought in a cup of tea. Manorama shut the book, reached out and took the cup. A shrivelled-up smile played on Kashi's lips.

'*Didi*, you mustn't take a servant's misdemeanour so seriously!' she said.

'You can save all that talk,' said Manorama crossly. 'Usually its enough to tick off a person just once, but with people like you nothing seems to sink in. Your children are content with chapati and dal but you need ghee for yourself. I'm sure such a mother would be unusual!'

It seemed by the expression on Kashi's face that someone had rent her apart. Her eyes were clouded with tears. '*Didi*, if it weren't for these children, you wouldn't have seen me alive today,' she declared. 'Unfortunately, one child was born when I'd been going hungry and he developed rickets. Now there's another on the way and God knows what disease he'll have to cope with!'

Manorama felt like someone had pushed her down from a height. Cold shivers ran down her body as she quickly gulped down her tea. She gazed at Kashi in astounded silence. 'Are you pregnant again?' she asked finally, as though this were something completely incredible.

Kashi's face bore a strange mixture of coquettishness and resignation. She nodded and glanced at the door with a deep sigh. Manorama had a fleeting vision of Ajudhya standing smiling before her. She finished her tea and put the cup down. Kashi carried it away. Manorama could feel her arms getting cold. She opened out the shawl and draped it lightly around her shoulders. Kashi returned inside. 'When would you like your dinner?' she asked.

Instead of replying, Manorama asked her, 'Did the doctor say the child will get well if he gets the ten injections?'

Kashi nodded silently and looked the other way.

'I'll give you twenty rupees,' said Manorama, rising from the chair. 'Go and get him injected tomorrow.'

She took out her wallet from the trunk and placed twenty rupees on the table. She wondered why her arms felt so cold. She hugged them tightly to herself.

After dinner she took a chair out on the veranda and sat there for a long time. Little sparks shot through her though she couldn't quite understand their nature and why she felt them in each pore of her being. They seemed to have no relation to anything outside but originated from deep within her, making her aware of the emptiness inside her. The deodar forest moaned in the strong wind. The wind howled and seemed to rise up in waves, engulfing her body, making her strangely helpless. She wrapped the shawl more tightly round herself.

The iron gate creaked as the wind pushed it. Her eyes closed for an instant and she imagined Ajudhya standing before her, dark lips parted in a smile, slowly tearing the iron gate open. She woke up with a start and a hand flew to her forehead. It was cold as ice. She stood up from the chair. Her shawl slipped off her shoulder in the process and the end of her sari fluttered like a bird in the breeze. Several tresses had escaped on to her forehead, caressing it.

'Kunti!' she called out in a feeble voice. Her voice drowned like a paper boat in the sea of wind.

'Kunti!' she repeated the cry. This time Kashi emerged from the quarter.

'Can you send Kunti to me if she's awake? I'd like her to sleep in my room tonight.' Even as she spoke, it struck Manorama how dependent she was on Kashi and her children and how much they needed her too.

'Kunti is asleep but I'll wake her up and send her to you at once,' said Kashi heading back.

'If she's asleep, let her be,' Manorama said as she walked back into her room from the veranda. Once inside, she shut the door as though she wanted to keep somebody out. She was overcome with extreme weakness. She pulled the quilt over herself and lay down. Her eyes travelled over the ceiling; she did not want to shut her eyes. As though she dreaded that the minute she did so, Ajudhya would stand there, smiling at her with his black lips.

To divert herself, she tried to form a tentative draft of what she would write to Sushil the next morning. Should she write that she was frightened of living alone and wanted to be with him? What about everything else she had experienced? Would she be able to tell him all that? Was it possible for her to explain why she felt so empty and what she expected from him to fill up this gap?

She had not brushed away the locks that had strayed on to her forehead. She was slowly becoming aware of their feathery touch. Soon it seemed to her that a tiny infant lay on the bed next to hers; his half-open lips resembled the soft new leaves of a mango tree and his silken hair blew into his face. She propped herself up on her elbow and gazed at the child . . . . Then she leaned over as though to kiss him.

THE CITY OF DEATH
Amarkant

Ram emerged from his house. He craned his head, rather like a crow, and looked around him with apprehension. The sky stretched like a clear blue tent above. The park in front, the houses and tree-tops, were bathed in glorious sunshine. By this time the locality would come alive and hum with a melodious din. No women or children were visible today, though. Just an ominous silence coiled like a snake, waiting to strike. Groups of two to four people stood before some houses; heads together, deep in conversation, like conspirators. Ram was a thin, middle-aged man; short-statured and somewhat squat. His shirt torn at the shoulder, crumpled pants giving the impression of pyjamas, swollen eyes streaked with red. He lifted his head and glanced up at the sky again and sighed deeply.

He advanced a few steps and paused. Visibly nervous, he pricked up his ears and cast a look around him. He thought he heard a great noise rising up from the adjacent locality and people running in his direction with shouts of 'Kill! Kill!' He imagined the glinting blade of a knife before his eyes. Should he run back inside? He fell back two steps. However, the people standing in front of the houses remained engrossed, as before, in conversation. Somewhat reassured, he tried to figure out what the commotion was all about, and, suddenly, everything became clear to him. Dogs were fighting in the locality nearby! Even dogs were at each other's throats these days! He tried to smile but the effort was short-lived, like a bubble.

It was going to be eight o'clock. Curfew had been lifted, after many days, for four hours in the morning and evening. He had just set out in the morning and his wife had pleaded, 'Do be careful!' Such was the state of his own fear, and, indeed, so alert was he, that anybody else's cautioning him appeared inauspicious. 'You're hoping something will happen to me!' he snapped. His wife burst into tears, and, once outside, he regretted having behaved like that, but in the general atmosphere of fear, his feeling got submerged like a pebble in a flood.

He picked up two more people from the neighbourhood on the way. This was apparently pre-planned. They moved forward. Looking at their pinched faces and the surreptitious glances they exchanged, one would have thought they had committed a crime!

'Anything special?' mumbled one of the three.

'A man has been stabbed near the railway station,' the other informed him.

'Is he a Hindu?'

'No, a Muslim.'

'Is it true that the body of a girl has been found in Himmatganj?'

'Yes.'

'Is she a Muslim?'

'No, a Hindu.'

Ram listened in silence. Someone was wringing the blood from his heart, he felt. Suddenly silence had fallen between them. A brick boundary wall continued for some distance from the point where the locality ended, perhaps in an effort to segregate people, but without success. The wall had been broken down at various places to allow for passage to the Muslim locality on the other side. After the country's independence, residents of both localities had lived harmoniously. They had worked at preserving relations with each other, the Hindus buying their milk from Muslim milkmen and the Muslims their provisions on credit from Hindu merchants. They met at weddings and also organized cricket and football matches against each other.

A boy called Jamil had become very popular in Ram's locality a couple of years ago. He loved drama and music. He had performed the role of Subhadra in the play *Veer Abhimanyu*, determined to render the part of a mythological Hindu woman very faithfully. He was so involved with his role that he collapsed and broke his head six times while mourning the death of Abhimanyu. This role had earned him fame as an authentic artist. Suddenly, however, all this had changed and people believed in nothing except murder, rumours and fear.

The three walked past the boundary wall, each trying to stay in the middle of the trio but none getting a stable measure of success. Ram, who was walking on the left, got a start when a young pandit walked up from behind. He wore a dhoti and banyaan and was barefoot. His plait waved in the air and his forehead was smeared with sandalwood. He had slipped into this locality to perform a religious ceremony when the curfew was lifted, and was now waiting to join others of his religion in order to walk back through the danger zone.

'I'll come along too . . . ,' he mumbled and made an unsuccessful attempt at smiling. He was determined to stay in the middle of the group as well. The momentum of movement jolted him around but he was back in the circle quickly like a mouse. This, at first, annoyed the others, but they soon realized the vulnerable predicament he was in, his attire rendering him the most easily recognizable as a Hindu.

The narrow lane was deserted—like the parting, devoid of vermilion, in a widow's hair. Ram had a faint memory, as of a dream remembered, that a few burqa-clad women were invariably seen on this road while children laughed shrilly and played in the dust. Kareeman, the wood shop owner's mother, was a familiar sight crossing the road or raucously calling out to her son, 'Ay! Shabbeer!' Young lads in loincloths would be seen bathing under the tap, after having a round in the wrestling ring. What self-confidence glowed from their eyes! However, only twenty to twenty-five people stood in front of a teashop now. They lifted angry eyes over bent heads, creating the impression that they stared with their eyebrows, lips twisted in a venomous smile.

The four began to walk faster, though there was no vigour in their legs. Their frames shook, rather like tazias. Past the hotel, they met five jawans of the Police Armed Constabulary on patrol. There was a Hindu settlement a little further down the road. Shacks of straw. Rubbish piled up haphazardly. The water in the drains had solidified and turned black. An ailing, elderly man sat outside his house, coughing violently. The pandit belonged to this locality. He detached himself from the group at this point and began to strut, chest thrust out.

'I walk alone on dark nights just like this!' He laughed, flashing his teeth.

Ram's friends took another road at the crossing and he was left alone. This was the same road that had hummed with life before, but the rickshaw pullers were not there today, nor were the men who repaired cycles while thronged by school and college boys on the pavement. Shops were shut as well. The hand-carts loaded with puffed rice and grams were not in sight, and those selling ice were missing too. Occasionally bands of dubious people approached from one direction and moved away into the other. Just now a group of Muslim labourers had walked up quickly from the right and disappeared to the left. How they jostled each other like cattle! Then they looked around alertly, in a manner reminiscent of dogs.

Ram moved forward resolutely, trying to gauge the situation. He turned and looked around now and then, like a jackal that had wandered into the city. He could perceive nothing but fear. He had never been in favour of such conflicts though he was not a coward. However, the unknown was an intimidating prospect which seemed to have drawn each drop of blood from his body. A poison had entered him, unawares, and it vitiated him gradually, making him feel small and inadequate. How horrifying was the desolation all round! Trivial sounds were echoing and gave the impression of tumultuous mobs. He really should not have ventured out today! But how could he have managed without? He worked in a little shop in the Civil Lines, and, lately, he had suffered a cut in his wages because of continual absence from work.

He arrived at a small Muslim dwelling. People standing before houses and shops glared at him with ferocious eyes. There were passers-by on the road as well. Ram felt numb with terror but kept moving nevertheless. He glanced round occasionally. Just then a youth ran up towards him from the left. His age could have been no more than twenty. Wearing knickers and a banyaan, he brandished a dagger. Ram saw him at once. The PAC jawans sat within hearing distance, but, frozen with terror, he momentarily lost his voice. The youth came running towards him but he ducked swiftly and escaped the thrust of the apprehended attack. The youth stared at him, then laughed and shot off into another alley like an unleashed arrow.

It was as if Ram had stopped breathing. He had even lost awareness of himself; was he walking or wasn't he? He could see himself dead. He found it difficult to tell whether he was muttering or his teeth were chattering. For an instant the faces of his wife and his sad children rose before his eyes.

Somebody else was advancing towards him now. He wore a lungi and a shirt.

He spoke, '*Babuji*, go straight ahead. You have no cause for worry. These outsiders give a bad name to the locality. This happened only because I was away. Usually I stand here and see to it that no incident takes place. Ah! What bad times! You buy milk from Majid, don't you?'

Ram tried to size him up with a careful look but could not figure him out. He wasn't trying to trick him, was he? He replied without pausing, 'Yes . . . .'

'Majid is my uncle. You go on ahead—don't worry. I'll tell you something though, *Babuji*. You shouldn't stir out of your house for the next couple of days. These are bad times . . .just walk on now . . . I'm watching over you . . . .'

Ram walked in a sort of daze. He could still feel the youth in the knickers pursuing him. Why had he laughed? His memory took him back to that time in high school when he had won a mile-long race dressed in just such knickers and a singlet.

He breathed a little easier when he reached the chowk. People were moving about, somewhat subdued. They kept at a distance from each other. You never could tell what might happen. Ram kept away from the others too. A few rickshaws stood by or circled round aimlessly. A rickshaw puller passed him yelling, 'Civil Lines, one seat!' The rickshaw's hood was pulled forward so he could not see the man sitting inside. He settled the fare and climbed into the rickshaw. However, he froze the minute he sat inside and looked around him. A bearded Muslim, hollow-cheeked and sunken-eyed, wearing a thin shirt and pyjamas, sat inside. He gazed at Ram in terror, though his expression also held a trace of rebellion against that terror.

The rickshaw jerked into motion. They clung to the edges of the rickshaw to prevent their bodies from touching, casting furtive looks at each other and then looking away again. Ram noticed that the bearded man's eyes often strayed to his waist and his pockets. He knew the reason for this, for he found himself glancing at the bearded man's waist occasionally too. When a bump on the road threw them together, they moved apart quickly and held on to their respective edges again.

Eight or ten people stood on the footpath in front of a hotel. A couple of them looked like wrestlers, wearing banyaans and red neckcloths. At a gesture from one of them, all the men fixed ferocious eyes on the rickshaw. 'Allah have mercy!' The words suddenly broke from the Muslim's mouth. Ram looked at him, startled. The bearded man had rested his forehead on the rickshaw's hood. His eyes were suspended above and his knees trembled badly. It did not take Ram long to work out what caused the man to behave like this. He was even a little reassured at the sight of this frightened man, who, so far, had been an object of fear for him. He wasn't going to die, was he? A short while ago, he had been in a similar state himself.

Ram shook the other's body. 'Listen. . . come to your senses. . . .'

The bearded man looked at him with extreme helplessness. No voice came from his mouth.

'Are you ill?'

'N-o,' he said indistinctly.

'Don't be frightened; there's nothing wrong,' Ram consoled him. The words escaped him unwittingly and they surprised him a little. He remembered that a few days ago he had been a human being. Indeed, a human being! Was it force of habit that had drawn these words from his mouth?

The rickshaw had moved forward. The bearded man was sitting up straight now. He had composed himself a little.

'What bad times these are!' he said.

'Yes, they are bad times, indeed,' Ram repeated.

'People are perishing like rats do with the plague!'

'Yes, both Hindus and Muslims are dying.'

'It's only the poor that get killed. I earn my bread every day. There's been nothing to eat in the house for three days.'

'Where do you work?' Ram asked.

'At the National Tailoring House. One can go hungry oneself, but it's difficult to see children starving! You can see that I was compelled to come out of my house today.'

'Yes, that's how things are . . . .'

'Women have abandoned their houses and run for their lives. Many of them are sharing a house, cooped up like hens. I can't describe their miserable condition. People are dying of hunger. Some are selling off their bicycles and watches. They've even pawned ornaments . . . .'

'Both sides are responsible.'

'Nobody is blameless. I've got a couple of Hindu friends, too, but they avoid me like the plague. And, frankly, I shy away from them too.'

'That is the root of the problem. That's why we never progress.'

'Yes, if we lived in harmony, nobody would dare to push us around.'

Suddenly they lapsed into silence. Their enthusiasm seemed to have waned. Ram had no desire to talk; in the same way that a sick man loses his appetite. The rickshaw sped on. They looked out in front. Every positive sentiment seemed so unnatural. Momentarily, Ram thought that the Muslim had agreed with him only to save his skin; that he didn't really mean it.

They had reached the Civil Lines. The bearded man had got the rickshaw to halt even before they reached the crossing. He paid his fare, and, without even a glance at Ram, he began to walk away. However, after going a few steps, he turned back. He had obviously remembered something. Coming back to Ram he smiled, as though he had some good news to impart. 'I wonder if I'll get back home tonight!. . . .well, goodbye . . . .Allah be willing we meet again.'

He turned and walked away briskly. He walked awry, as though he were a leaf tossed in the wind. Ram's rickshaw moved forward. He got off at the crossroad too. Tears dimmed his eyes. He found it difficult to tell what brought on the tears; gratitude to the Muslim or his own feeling of helplessness? Yet the contemplation of this sadness afforded him a certain pleasure. Fear had clouded his perception of happiness and sorrow, but the man had evoked a feeling of sadness deep within him. Only a short while ago he'd thought him a murderer, but he had turned out to be a lamb. Majid's relative had been like that too. . . .

Past the crossroad, Ram emerged on the street ahead. He looked around him joyfully. Beautiful roads and shops. Green trees.Then he remembered that he had to return home in the evening and a burden settled on him. His heart began to sink again. A strong wind had risen, carrying with it a woman's lament, or was it children moaning? Suddenly a koel began to sing on a tree. The cooing of a koel! Since the outbreak of the riot the koel must have sung many times, but he'd never noticed it before. Now, however, he could hear its song clearly.

APPREHENSION
Kunwar Narayan

He entered the room, dangerous and dirty insect that he was, and made himself comfortable on my papers. Perhaps he intended to nibble them away. I had an urge to pick him up and fling him outside. But he was extremely repulsive. I considered getting a servant to throw him out; and if a single servant were insufficient, then many servants. Maybe he guessed my intention. It was surprising, though, that even this did not scare him. Looking at this frail object, I could not fathom the source of his evil courage. The sight of my angry face did not seem to make a difference to his brazen confidence either. In fact, his shameless audacity grew visibly. He gazed at me as though confident that I could do nothing to harm him, whereas, if he so wished, he could annihilate me in an instant by a flick of his fingers. The thought that such a beast possessed the strength to destroy a human being like me, filled my heart with a bitter despair.

So far he had made no display of power, yet his existence gradually acquired the form of an irrational terror. He and I were the only two occupants of that room, yet he somehow gave the impression that it was solely he who possessed knowledge as to who presented the greater danger to the other. As I saw it, he should, in any case, have kept away from me, because no relationship, except that of hatred, was possible between us. The very fact of his proximity to me was a warning that I should be on my guard against danger of one kind or another.

Suddenly he moved from his place and reached the door. The door was shut. This appeared to reassure him. The manner in which he walked seemed to me to be a bad omen. Perhaps one of his legs was slightly defective, because he limped a little, somewhat like a crab. He seemed to disturb the entire atmosphere as he walked, and, I noticed, for the first time, that, because of his presence, a strange smell of flesh had filled the room. It was an unfamiliar odour; one which I associated, in some context or the other, with violence and bestiality. It brought home, too, the fact that he had lived mainly amongst ferocious beings and would perhaps be quite alien to human virtues like mercy and sympathy. In order to resolve situations he would only resort to the primitive techniques of attack and defence. His first reaction to anything unfamiliar would be the same as any other wild animal's—that is, to prick up his ears with suspicion. Then he would concentrate his attention on trying to assess the intruder's strength. If, he found him to be the weaker, he would very cleverly, and with great stealth, jump on him and destroy him. If, on the other hand, the intruder was discovered to be the stronger of the two, he would employ all his faculties and take to his heels.

He returned and concentrated his energies on the papers once more. I noticed that he appeared to be interested only in the sheets that had been written on and not in the blank ones. It was, therefore, apparent that his attention was focused on the ink and not on the paper. He would give every letter a trial lick but it seemed he did not care for most of them; perhaps he did not find what he was after. I had fixed my attention on his cruel red eyes that were riveted on the paper. Looking at those eyes, it was difficult to believe that his diet could be paper; indeed, the single-mindedness with which he scanned the writing could only have been levelled at things that could be killed and not merely written.

It was not as though he did not find a single paper that he fancied. He was keeping some papers aside, perhaps with an unclear intention. It was possible, too, that he did not care much for those papers either, but was having to make do with them for lack of anything better.

It had become quite clear by now that he was, in fact, not as weak as he looked. He did not have a very big frame, it was true, but he was certainly possessed of a secret strength, banking on which he sat there so arrogantly before me—perhaps venomous fangs in his mouth or concealed claws that were sharp and deadly, like those of cats. Maybe, like a hippopotamus or a boar, he was relying on his thick hide. It was possible, too, that he possessed hard armour, like a tortoise, within which he could immediately take shelter when he was attacked. However, I quickly dismissed this idea, because, to my mind, no one would come to me expecting to be attacked. More likely, he would be the aggressor. Again, it did not seem, from the way in which he behaved, that he was frightened of me. Indeed, his bearing was such that I should have been scared of him.

Without a doubt, he repeatedly presented himself in such a fashion as to provoke me into attacking him, and thus give him an opportunity to evince his concealed strength. My heart was consumed by an unbearable anger at the carelessness with which he scattered the papers about. I was trying my utmost to assess his actual strength, for, by now, I was convinced that I had committed a fatal error in assuming that he was weaker than I. This conclusion had an adverse effect on me, as I found that I was extremely nervous.

Till now I had considered myself safe from hazards of this sort because I kept away from them, but I now realized that my staying away from them had no meaning. I was safe only to the extent that they kept away from me. I could not tuck myself away in such a fashion that, as a consequence of my schemes, diminutive insects, possibly poisonous, could not get to me. Nor could my schemes be so enduring that they could withstand the concerted onslaught of many large insects. The degree of my safety depended not so much on me as on others, particularly on their circumspection; and if one did not want to understand a human being in the light of humanity, that person's misfortune was limitless.

I was bracing myself to meet every possible danger, for that which I confronted at this point inspired no faith in humanity. I felt that I stood before a creature that was half beast and half machine, from whom it was futile to hope for any kind of deliverance.

I started up from where I sat but then decided not to get up, perhaps in an attempt to check what effect this would have on him. He just sat there, completely untouched by this, getting on with his work, as though he were fully aware of my limitations. Instead of being resolved or diminished, my discomfiture mounted. It had become imperative now to resolve the situation in one way or another, even should the resolution prove harmful for me.

Finally, prepared to the teeth, I stood up. I had decided I would first open the door, call the servant and then proceed. It was necessary to feel completely secure. The fact that I had stood up brought about no change in his manner. It was possible that he laughed at my childish efforts. Saying nothing to him, I moved towards the door. For the first time he turned his head around and glared at me harshly, as though to tell me to sit down quietly in my place or else! For the first time I too tried to give him the impression that there was no way his threats were going to work on me.

He silently stared at me, as though I were an extremely naïve and pathetic thing, pretending to feel pity for this creature's futile endeavours. I paused at the door for an instant to see whether he would do anything. He turned his head in disdain and looked, or pretended to look, at the papers once again. I opened the door in annoyance.

The minute I opened the door, I started to a halt. The secret fear in my heart became a reality. He had not come alone. The door was completely surrounded. At a single gesture, they could crawl into the room and trample over me and my papers, in fact, over my entire world. There I was, totally helpless, so much so that I could not have called out to my servant. I volunteered a guess, which proved correct, that many more surrounded my house than stood at the door; and many more than those were in the town, outside the town, in the country, in the world . . . there was no way I could get rid of them. I could not flee from them either. If they so desired, they could unite and finish me off at once. Maybe a faint scream would issue from my mouth; perhaps not even that. Perhaps I would prefer to pass away silently, like a sage or a scientist belonging to a bygone age, along with my blameless writings.

THE GUEST
Nirmal Verma

He kept his suitcase down in front of the door, pressed the doorbell and waited. The house was silent; there was no sign of life. He had a momentary illusion that the house was deserted. Taking out a handkerchief he wiped off his perspiration, then placed his air-bag on the suitcase. He rang the bell again and listened, his ear pressed to the door. Behind the veranda an open window swung in the breeze.

He moved back a little and looked up. The house was two-storeyed; not very different from other houses in the lane—black roof slanting down in a V shape, supported in the centre by a white stone wall, the number of the house shining on its brow like a black bindi. The upstairs windows were shut and the curtains drawn. Where could they have gone at this hour?

He walked round to the back of the house—the lawn, fences and hedges had not changed much in the two years that had passed since he'd last seen them. A willow with drooping branches dozed like an old black bear in the midst of it all. The garage, however, was open and empty; they had gone somewhere in the car. It was possible that they had gone out for something after having waited for him through the morning. But, surely, they could have left a note for him at the door.

He returned to the front door. The discomfiting light of August pricked his eyes. He was drenched in sweat. Sitting down on his suitcase in the veranda he soon became aware of faces peering at him from the windows across the street. The English were not inquisitive; they left one alone, he had heard; though he was sitting in the veranda outside the house, where the right to privacy probably didn't extend. Perhaps that was why they stared at him unabashed, with naked fascination. Or maybe their curiosity could be explained in another way. In that little suburban English town almost every body knew the other, and here he was, undoubtedly peculiar looking, dressed as he was in an ill-fitting Indian suit. His crumpled, worn clothes and grimy face bathed in sweat made it impossible to guess that three days ago he had read out a paper at a conference in Frankfurt. 'I probably look like a decrepit Asian immigrant . . . ,' he thought and stood up suddenly, as though standing made the waiting easier. This time he knocked quite involuntarily and stepped back, startled, when the door clicked open. Footsteps sounded on the stairs and then she stood there, on the threshold.

She'd come running down the stairs and had hugged him. Before he could ask 'Were you inside?' or, indeed, before she could ask 'Were you standing outside?' he grasped her thin shoulders with his dust-laden, clumsy hands, and, as the girl's head bent forward, he buried his face in her hair.

One after the other the neighbours shut their windows. The girl moved him away gently. 'How long have you been standing outside?'

'The last two years.'

'Go on!' The girl laughed. She found her father so clownish when he spoke like this.

'I rang the bell twice—where were you?'

'It's out of order; that's why I'd left the door open.'

'You could have told me that on the phone—I've been running around for the past hour.'

'I was about to when the line got disconnected . . . .why didn't you put in more money?'

'I only had ten pence . . . .that woman was a bitch!'

'Which woman?' The girl picked up his bag.

'The operator who cut us short in the middle of our conversation.'

The man dragged his suitcase into the living-room. The girl was looking into the bag eagerly—cigarettes, a large bottle of Scotch, bundles of chocolates; all the things he'd bought hurriedly, from the duty free shop at Frankfurt airport, were now peeping out from it.

'Have you had a haircut?' For the first time he looked carefully at the girl's face.

'Yes . . . just for the duration of my holidays. How does it look?'

'If you weren't my daughter, I'd have thought a tramp had forced his way into the house.'

'Oh! Papa!' The girl laughed as she picked up a chocolate from the bag, tore the wrapper and offered it to him. 'Swiss chocolate!' she said, waving it in the air.

'Can you get me a glass of water?'

'Wait a minute, I'll make some tea for you.'

'The tea can wait . . . .' He fumbled inside his coat pocket—notebook, wallet, passport—and, last of all, the little container of pills he had been looking for.

Returning with the glass of water, the girl asked him, 'What kind of medicine is it?'

'German,' he said. 'It's very effective.' He gulped down the pill with some water and sat down on the sofa. It was just as he had imagined it—that room, the glass door and the square lawn resembling a green handkerchief—visible through the curtains pulled aside, the reflection of birds in flight on the television screen; birds that flew outside but appeared to be within.

He walked to the threshold of the kitchen. He could see the girl behind the gas cookers, her back towards him. Black corduroy jeans and white shirt whose rolled-up sleeves swung near her elbows. She looked infinitely frail, as though she would wilt at a touch.

'Where is Mama?' he asked her. Perhaps his voice was so low she did not hear him, yet he felt her neck lift a little. 'Is Mama upstairs?' he repeated, but the girl stood motionless and he realized that she had heard his question the first time. 'Has she gone out?' he asked.

There was a faint movement of the girl's head, which could have meant anything.

'Papa, will you help me?'

He leaped forward into the kitchen. 'Tell me, what do you need done?'

'Will you take the teapot into the drawing-room? I'm just coming.'

'Is that all?' he asked, disappointed.

'Okay, you can take the cups and saucers as well.'

He carried everything into the living-room. He felt like going back into the kitchen but remained where he was because he wasn't sure she'd approve. He could smell something frying in the kitchen. She was cooking something for him, and here he was, unable to help her in any way. He wanted to go in there and stop her; he wouldn't eat—but just then he realized that he was very hungry. He had eaten nothing since morning. There had been a long queue at the Euston station cafeteria, so he had just bought his ticket and boarded the train. He'd eat something in the dining-car, he had decided—but it turned out that it did not open till afternoon. In fact, his last meal had been at Frankfurt airport, and when he reached London at night, he'd sat in the bar of his hotel, drinking. After his third drink he had taken out his notebook, located the number and dialled from the telephone booth . . . . At first he couldn't tell whether it was his wife or the child. Then the silence echoing at the other end had told him it was his wife. He heard her call the child from upstairs. Looking at his watch he suddenly realized she must have been asleep. He had an impulse to hang up but just then he heard the child's voice. She sounded very sleepy. For some time she could not tell whether he spoke from India or Frankfurt or London. . . .Three minutes were over before he'd been able to explain his situation to her and he did not even have the change to keep the line going. He had the consolation, anyway, of having told her, despite the nervous, sleepy and inebriated state he was in, that he would reach their place tomorrow . . . that is, today.

Now he felt fine. The pale English sun was out, spreading a mellow radiance. He sat inside the room, feeling waves of warmth surging within him. Hurrying to airports, checking in and out of hotels, the frantic haste to board trains on time—he was away from it all now. He was inside a house; not his own, it was true, but certainly a home—with chairs, curtains, sofas, a TV. He had lived among these things for years and every object held a familiar association. When he returned every two or three years, he wondered how big the child had grown; and his wife?

She must certainly have changed. Yet these objects stayed the way they were. He carried a memory of them when he left and came back years later to find them just the same.

'Papa, didn't you pour the tea?' She came in from the kitchen carrying two plates—butter and toast in one and fried sausages in the other.

'I was waiting for you.'

'Pour it before it gets cold,' she said settling down on the sofa beside him.

'Do you want me to turn on the TV? . . . . Is there anything you'd like to watch?'

'Not now. . . . listen, did you get the stamps I sent you?'

'Yes, Papa, thank you!' She was buttering some toast.

'You didn't write a single letter though!'

'I did, but I got your wire just then and didn't think there was any point in sending it since you were coming.'

'You are a goat!'

The girl looked at him and laughed. This was a nickname her father had given her years ago, when they all lived together. She was very little then and had never heard of India.

Taking advantage of her laughter, he bent over her as though she were a lively bird that could only be caught in an illusory moment of security. 'When will Mummy be back?'

The question was so sudden it took the girl unawares. 'She's upstairs in her room,' she blurted.

'Upstairs? But you said. . . .'

Scrunch, scrunch, scrunch—she was scraping away the burnt bits of toast, and, it seemed to him, his question too. She was still smiling, but now the smile seemed stuck to her lips, like a frozen insect.

'Does she know I'm here?'

The girl spread butter and jam on the toast and slid the plate across to him.

'Yes, she does,' she said.

'Won't she come downstairs and have tea with us?'

The girl began to rearrange the sausages on the other plate—then, remembering something, she went into the kitchen and returned with mustard and ketchup.

'I'll go upstairs and ask her.' He looked at the girl as though to get her approval. Seeing that she said nothing, he moved towards the stairs.

'Please, Papa!'

His steps faltered.

'Do you want to fight with her again?' The girl looked at him a shade angrily.

'Fight!' He broke into an embarrassed laugh. 'Do you think I've come two thousand miles to fight with her?'

'Why don't you sit here with me then?' the girl implored. She was protective of her mother but not short on sympathy for her father. She glanced at him reassuringly, as though to say, 'I'm here with you; isn't that enough?'

He began to eat sausages, toast and boiled tinned peas. He'd lost his appetite but he could feel the girl's eyes on him. She looked at him, preoccupied. Occasionally she bit off some toast and sipped her tea. Then she smiled up at him, as if consoling him: 'It's all right, so long as I'm with you, there is nothing to fear.'

It wasn't fear, though. It could have been the effect of the pills, or perhaps the fatigue of the journey was catching up with him now—he wanted to be by himself, to get away. 'I'm just coming,' he said.

The girl darted a suspicious look at him. 'Going to the toilet?' She accompanied him, and, even when he'd shut the door, he could feel her standing there.

He bent his face over the wash-basin and turned the tap. Water gushed over his face—a kind of sob escaped him and incoherent words rushed out from the hollow of his heart, as though he were vomiting moss that had accumulated there. The pill he had swallowed just before was now a yellow mess in the marble sink. Then he turned off the tap and wiped his face on a handkerchief.

A woman's dirty clothes hung on a hook in the bathroom . . . his eyes travelled over underwear soaking in a big plastic bucket . . . through the open window, the rear portion of the garden glittered in the sunlight. The sleepy hum of a lawn mower was audible from some other garden . . . .

He shut the bathroom door quickly and came back into the room. The house was silent. The girl was not in the kitchen, and the drawing-room, too, was empty. He suspected she was upstairs with her mother. A strange terror caught hold of him. The infinitely tranquil house seemed fraught with much danger. He walked over to his suitcase in the corner and flung it open hurriedly. Setting aside his conference notes and papers, he pulled out the stuff underneath them that he had bought from Delhi—a Rajasthani skirt from an emporium (for the girl), brass and copper trinkets from the Tibetan shops on Janpath, a Kashmiri pashmina shawl (for the girl's mother), red Gujarati brocade slippers that both the child and the mother could wear, handloom bedcovers, an album of Indian stamps and an enormous picture book titled *Banaras: the Eternal City*. Gradually, a miniature India, one that he carried with him each time he visited them, had grown up on the floor.

His hands faltered as his eyes took in the scene. The things scattered about on the floor looked destitute and somehow pitiful. He had a mad instinct to leave everything on the floor and run. Nobody would have an inkling as to where he'd gone. The girl would no doubt wonder; but over the years she had got used to his sudden comings and equally unexpected departures. She would not be more than ordinarily sad at not finding him there. She would go upstairs to her mother and say, 'You can come downstairs now; he's gone.' Then they would come down together, relieved that there was no one else in the house.

'Papa!'

He jumped, as though caught red-handed. He smiled sheepishly at the girl who stood in the doorway gazing at the open suitcase as if it were a magic box that had suddenly emitted colourful things. Her eyes held only dismay, though. There was no hint of joy in them. As though she had caught out a grown-up trick, one whose secret she already knew, and displayed an exaggerated enthusiasm to cover up her embarrassment.

'Such a lot of things!' She sat down in the chair in front of him. 'How did they allow you to bring them? I've heard the Customs really harass one these days.'

'No, this time they said nothing!' the man said with a hint of triumph in his voice. 'Perhaps because I came in straight from Frankfurt. They were not sure about one thing though . . . .' He winked at the girl.

'And what was that?' This time the girl was genuinely curious.

He opened a box of salted peas and placed it on the table.

The girl picked up a few grains and smelt them hesitantly. 'What's this?' She looked at him curiously.

'They smelt it like that too.' He laughed. 'They were scared it might contain hash.'

'Hash?' The girl's eyes widened. 'Does it really have hash in it?'

'Well, eat it and find out!'

The girl put some of the grains in her mouth and munched cautiously, but soon grew agitated, making hissing, sucking sounds.

'It must be the chillies—spit it out!' said the man urgently.

The girl, however, had already swallowed them and looked at her father, her eyes flowing.

'You were crazy to swallow all of that!' the man exclaimed, quickly handing her the glass of water she had brought for him.

'I like it.' The girl gulped down the water and wiped her eyes with the folded sleeve of her shirt. Then she gave him a smile and said, 'I love it.' There were many things she said just to make him happy. They had very little time together and she used many short-cuts to reach him, to cover a distance other children would traverse in months.

'Did they taste it as well?'

'No, they dared not! They just undid my suitcase, fumbled about with my papers, and, when they discovered that I was coming from a conference, they said, "Mister, you may go".'

'What did they say?' laughed the girl.

'They said "Mister, you may go, like an Indian crow!" The man looked at her with a secretive glint in his eyes. 'What is this?' The girl was still laughing. They had played this absurd game when she had been very little and they had gone for walks together in the park. He would look at a tree and ask, 'Oh dear, is there anything to see?' Then the girl would look around her carefully and say, 'Yes dear, there is a crow over the tree.' The man would throw her an astonished look. 'What is this?' he'd ask. She would laugh triumphantly and say, 'A poem!'

A poem! Shadows of a fleeting childhood slid over his advancing years—the breeze in the park, trees, laughter. Holding on to her father's finger, she had come to a place she had left behind ages ago, which appeared in her dreams once in a while . . . .

'I brought some Indian coins for you. . . remember you asked me for them the last time?'

'Show me, where are they?' the girl was perhaps a shade too enthusiastic.

The man picked up a red-beaded purse—the kind that hippies use for carrying their passports in. The girl snatched it from his hand and waved it in the air. The four and eight-anna bits began to clink and jingle. Then she opened the mouth of the bag and poured the coins on the table.

'Does every one in India have coins like these?'

He laughed. 'Do you think they manufacture different coins for every one?' he asked.

'But what about the poor people?' She gazed at him reflectively. 'I saw them one night on television.' She had forgotten about the coins and was looking at the things scattered on the floor, a little baffled.

For the first time the man got the feeling that the girl sitting before him was not the same person that he knew. The frame within which he recognized her was the same, but the picture had changed. Perhaps she had not changed at all; she had simply gone somewhere else. Parents who do not live with their children know little about the secret habitations that are built on the desert of their deprivation. The girl could meet her father only in the safe corners that held her childhood ... though she occasionally strayed to other corridors the man knew absolutely nothing about.

'Papa!' The girl looked at him. 'Should I pick up these things and put them away?'

'Why, what's the hurry?'

'No, there's no hurry, but if Mama comes and sees them ... !' Her tone held a vague apprehension, as though she smelt an unseen fear in the air.

'What if she does come?' The man shot a slightly puzzled look at her.

'Papa, talk softly ... .' The girl glanced up at the room above. There was silence upstairs, as though the house had been split into two, one half of which lay numb and motionless while they sat in the other. Then he had the illusion that the girl was playing a game of puppets. Suspended from a string above, the girl moved with each pull, though he could see neither the string nor the person who controlled it ... .

He stood up.

The girl looked at him in terror. 'Where are you going?'

'Won't she come downstairs?' he asked.

'She knows you're here.'

'Is that why she doesn't want to come?'

'No ... !' said the girl. 'That's why she could come any moment.'

How foolish he was! He couldn't understand such a simple thing. 'Sit down, won't you? I'll just put these things in order.' Squatting down on the floor she stacked everything away in a corner neatly—the velvet shoe, the fur shawl, the bedcover from the Gujarat emporium. She had her back to him, but he could see her hands, dusky and thin like her mother's, and as cold and aloof; hands that did not lovingly handle the gifts he'd brought, but shoved them into a corner indifferently. They were the hands of a child secure within the familiar bounds of a mother's love; a stranger to the eager, pained passion that wells out from the dark cavern of a father's love.

Suddenly the girl's hands paused. She thought someone rang the doorbell, but the next instant she remembered the telephone in the alcove under the stairs. It was screaming like a chained puppy. The girl left the things for the moment and leapt towards the telephone. At first he heard nothing, then she yelled out, 'Mama, a call for you!'

She stood there, leaning against the banister, the receiver swinging from her hand. The upstairs door opened and the stairs trembled under the weight of someone descending. A head bent over the girl—a plaited bun—and then a whole face rose into view next to the phone.

'Who is it?' The woman pushed back her loose bun and pulled the phone from the girl's hand. The girl looked at the man as he rose from the chair . . . . 'Hello,' said the woman. 'Hello, hello,' rose her voice and he realized that the voice belonged to the woman who was his wife. He could have recognized it years later, over a babble of voices . . . trembling slightly at a high pitch, constant in its severity, always injured, bewildered. It was the single thing in her body that had the capacity to rend the flesh and scratch a trail of blood on a man's spirit . . . he sat down just as he had stood up.

The girl was smiling. She looked at the man's face in the mirror on the wall and it seemed as clumsy as the voice of the woman in the mirror of age—distorted, awry, mysterious like a riddle! The three, unknown to themselves, had split into four; the girl and her mother; the man and his wife. In the process of acquiring domesticity, a house spreads itself out involuntarily.

'Will you talk to Jenny?' the woman asked the girl who seemed to be waiting for just this moment. She jumped up on to the stairs and took the receiver from her mother. 'Hello, Jenny, it's me!'

The woman climbed down two steps and the man could now see all of her.

'Do sit down . . . .' The man rose. His voice acquired a tone of helpless appeal, as though he feared she would turn back as soon as she saw him.

She stood, undecided for a moment. Turning back now was meaningless; yet there was no point in standing like that before him either. She pulled up a stool and sat down in front of the TV.

'When did you come?' The voice was so low that the man felt it had been another woman who had spoken on the phone.

'Quite a while ago . . . I had no idea you were upstairs!' The woman looked at him quietly. The man took out a handkerchief from his pocket, wiped off his sweat and made an effort to smile.

'I stood outside for a long time; I didn't know the bell was out of order! The garage was empty so I thought you'd both gone out . . . . Where's your car though?' He knew the answer already, but asked anyway.

'It's gone to be serviced!' said the woman. She had always hated these trivial, inane things he said; whereas, for the man, they were straws to be clutched at, to save himself from drowning. At least for a while . . . .

'Did you get my wire? I'd come to Frankfurt and got the same ticket extended. I just had to pay a few pounds extra. I called you from there but you'd both gone out . . . .'

'When?' asked the woman, a little curious. 'We've both been home.'

'The bell kept ringing but no one picked up the phone. Maybe the operator couldn't figure out my English and gave me a wrong number! But listen!' He laughed, 'Something strange happened. I saw a woman at Heathrow who looked just like you from behind. I'm glad I didn't call out to her . . . all Indian women look the same when they are outside India . . . .' He was talking incessantly. He was like a man who walks a tightrope blindfolded. The woman stood somewhere much below, in a dream. He had known her long ago but he could no longer remember why he sat before her now . . . .

He grew silent. He suddenly realized he'd been listening to his own voice all this while; the woman sat absolutely quiet. She cast cold, despairing glances at him.

'What is the matter?' asked the man a little apprehensively.

'Why don't you understand? I told you I don't want anything from you . . . why do you bring these things to my house? What's the use?'

At first he was confused about what she meant. Then his eyes travelled to the floor . . . the Shantiniketan purse, the stamp album, the box of salted peas—lying pell-mell on the floor the things looked forlorn and pathetic in the same way that he did sitting on the chair.

'It's not much . . . ,' he said peevishly. 'Not even half a suit-case . . . .'

'I just don't want anything at all from you . . . can't you under-stand this simple little fact?' Her voice rose and trembled, fraught with the pain of countless quarrels, bursting through the dam that held back hellish waters dark with agonizing memories.

'Can't you stand even such a short visit?'

'No. . . .' Her face tensed up and then loosened into a strange resignation. 'I don't want to see you again . . . that's all!'

As if that were easy! He looked at her like an obstinate boy, pretending not to understand even when everything was perfectly clear to him.

'Bukku!' he said softly, 'please!'

'Oh, no! Not that all over again!' said the woman.

'What is it that you want?'

'Leave me alone . . . that's all I want!'

'Can't I come even to meet the child?'

'Not in this house. You'll have to meet her somewhere outside.'

'Outside?' the man raised his head, baffled. 'Where?' He forgot for a moment that the entire world lay outside; parks, streets, hotel-rooms—his own world—could he drag the child everywhere?

His daughter was laughing into the telephone: 'No, I can't come today. Papa's here; he's just come . . . no, I don't know. I didn't ask him . . . .' What didn't she know? Perhaps her friend had asked her how long he would stay. The woman sitting before him, too, was perhaps eager to find out how much time, how many hours of torture would she yet have to undergo with him.

The last rays of the afternoon sun filtered into the room, the TV screen reflecting their glow. The image of the woman sat in its blankness, resembling the form of a news reader, blurred to begin with, gradually growing brighter . . . . He waited with bated breath for her to say something, knowing all the while that the past could only play again the worn-out tape of pain relating to another life . . . how different were things from people! The house, books, rooms—they remained the same as you left them years ago; but people began to die away the day they were separated . . . indeed, they did not die but moved into another life which slowly stifled the one you led together . . . .

'It was not just the child . . . ,' he stammered. 'I came to meet you too.'

'Me?' The woman's face simultaneously mirrored derision, disdain and astonishment. 'You still haven't lost your habit of telling lies, have you?'

'What would I get by lying to you now?'

'I don't know what you'll get—I only know what I've got out of it.' She fixed a cool, steadfast gaze outside. 'If I'd known about you from before, I could have done something.'

'What could you have done?' A cold tremor swept through him.

'Anything . . . I can't stay alone like you. But now, at this age . . . no one even looks at me.'

'Bukku! . . .' he caught her hand.

'Don't take my name . . . all that's over now.'

She was weeping; completely alone, as detached from the griefs of the past as from hopes for the future. The dam having given way, her tears gushed down like a torrent over her undulating life. She brushed them away with a jerk of her hand. The child sat motionless on the last step, by the phone, watching her weeping mother with dry eyes. All her efforts had proved fruitless, yet her face showed no despair. Every family has its nightmares that spin like an endless wheel; she knew better than to dabble with them. At such a tender age she had grasped the truth that there was a strange co-relation between man's heart inside and the cycle of fate which wheels around the world outside—that there was no way to stop it midway.

She went over to her mother without glancing at the man. She said something to her which was obviously not meant for him. The woman pulled her down—very close to her. They looked like two sisters, sitting there on the couch like that. They had forgotten about him. The tide that had submerged the house a short while ago had subsided, leaving the man where he should have been—on the shore. He had a feeling that this was a lifelong wish that had been granted to him by God; there he sat in their midst—invisible! God alone is invisible in his mercy—he knew this. Yet, the man who lives in the lowest layer of the pit may not be visible either. The mother and daughter had left him alone—though, without an intention to demean him. Turning away from him they'd left him to his own devices—just the way he had left the house years ago.

Moving away from her mother at last, the girl sat down near him. 'Will you come and see our garden?' she asked.

'Now?' he looked at the girl, a little dismayed. She seemed eager and somehow restless, as though she had some thing to say which she could not possibly communicate in the room.

'Okay, let's go,' said the man, getting up. 'But take these things upstairs first.'

'Oh, we can sort them out later!'

'Later? When?'

'Come on!' The girl almost dragged him.

'Tell him to put his things back in the suitcase.' The woman's voice was cold, measured.

It was as though someone had pushed him from behind. He jerked around. 'Why?'

'I don't need them.'

A furious storm was brewing within him. 'I won't take them back; you can throw them outside if you like.'

'Outside?' The woman's voice quivered. 'I can throw you outside with them too.'

Her eyes sparkled after the bout of tears. The wetness on her cheeks had set like brittle glass, her face stained with tears that had not been wiped, but left to dry.

'Won't we go to see the garden?' The child pulled at his hand and he began to walk with her. He saw nothing, though. The grass, flower-beds and trees moved like a dumb film. All he heard was his wife's voice echoing like a ghostly commentary—outside, outside!

'Why do you argue with Mummy?' asked the girl.

'You think I argue with her, do you?' he shot a wounded look at the girl as though she, too, were his enemy.

'Yes, you do!' Her tone was tinged with defiance. When she was cross with him she reverted from the intimate form of address to the more formal one. The uncertainty of the English pronoun suspended the relationship between father and daughter in mid-air, swinging from close to very distant and he could only get an idea of its measure by the tone she used. The man found himself possessed by a strange fear. He did not want to lose the mother and the child all at once.

'It's a lovely garden,' he cajoled. 'Do you have a gardener?'

'No, there's no gardener,' the girl spoke with enthusiasm. 'I water it in the evening and Mummy mows the lawn when she has a day off . . . come here, I'll show you something.'

He fell into step behind her. It was a very small lawn, smooth like yellow-green velvet. The garage was round the back, flanked by a hedged fence on both sides. A thick old willow stood in the middle. Partly concealed behind the tree, the girl called out, 'Where are you?' He crept forward silently and then stood amazed. Between the willow and the fence was a black wooden enclosure—a rabbit peeped out of the door while the girl held another rabbit, caressing it rather like it were a ball of wool that could drop from her hands any minute and get lost in the bushes.

'We got these a few days ago . . . there were two to begin with, now there are four!'

'Oh, really? Where are the rest?'

'In the enclosure . . . they are very little just now.'

He had an urge to stroke the rabbit, too, but his hand travelled to the girl's head of its own accord and he began to play gently with her short, dark hair. The girl stood silently while the rabbit looked at her, crinkling up its nose.

'Papa?' the girl spoke softly without raising her head, 'have you bought a day-return ticket?'

'No, why?'

'I just asked; because you can get cheap return tickets here.'

Was it for this that she'd called him outside? His hand moved away from the girl's head slowly.

'Listen, where do you plan to spend the night?' The girl's voice was quite devoid of expression.

'And what if I stay here?'

The girl put the rabbit back in the enclosure gently and clicked the door shut.

'I was only joking!' He laughed. 'I'll take the last train back.'

The girl turned her head to look at him. 'There are a couple of good hotels here too . . . . I'll ring them in a minute and find out for you.' The girl's voice was inflected with tenderness. Having confirmed that he would not spend the night there, she had left her mother's side and come over to him; she took his hand gently and stroked it, much as she had caressed the rabbit a short while ago. The man's hand, however, was moist with perspiration.

'Listen, I'm coming to India in my next vacation—this time it's quite certain.' She wanted to please him.

She was a little surprised when the man said nothing. The pattering of the rabbits inside the enclosure was all they could hear.

'Papa . . . why don't you say something? Wouldn't you like me to come to India?'

'Oh . . . ! That's what you promise every year.'

'I know I do . . . but this year I'll definitely make it. Don't you believe me?'

'Shall we go back inside? Your mother must be wondering where we've gone to.'

The August darkness had stolen up. The willow leaves rustled in the wind. The curtains had been drawn though the kitchen door was open. Running inside, the girl turned on the tap and began to wash her hands in the sink. He stood behind her. His haggard face looked back at him from the mirror above the sink—grimy, with an overgrown beard and bloodshot eyes . . . no, there was no hope for him . . . .

'Papa, do you still talk to yourself?' The girl lifted up her wet face to gaze at his reflection in the mirror.

'Yes, I do, but no one listens to me now . . . .'

He placed a gentle hand on the girl's shoulder. 'Is there any soda in the fridge?'

'Yes, of course, you carry on inside—I'll go and get you some.'

He retreated to the lonely living-room. His things had been collected together. His suitcase stood in a corner. His wife must have looked at the things when they were out in the garden; touched them too, perhaps. Though she was angry with him, it was a different matter when it came to things. She hadn't taken them upstairs, it was true, but had not put them back in the suitcase, either . . . she'd left them to their fate.

Just for a moment he could not remember where he was when the child returned with the soda and a glass a short while later. It was dark in the room; dark enough for the man who sat in the midst of those objects to look like an object too.

'Papa . . . why didn't you switch on the light?'

'Well, I'll put it on now . . . .' He rose and fumbled for the switch. The girl placed the soda and the glass on the table and lit the table lamp.

'Where's Mummy?'

'She's in the shower; she'll come soon.'

He took out the whisky that he had bought at the Frankfurt airport from his bag . . . his hands paused as he poured it into the glass. 'Where's your ginger-ale?'

'Oh, I drink real beer now!' The girl laughed up at him. 'Do you want some ice?'

'No . . . but where are you going?'

'To feed the rabbits . . . or they'll end up feeding on each other!'

When she went out, the darkness of the garden was visible through the open door—glimmering with the pale glow of the stars. There was no breeze. The silence outside filtered through the unseen sounds of the house. He had a feeling he sat in his own house and every thing was the same as it had been years ago. She would be humming under the shower, and, when she emerged, with a towel tied on her head like a turban, the drops dripping from her hair would etch a trail from the bathroom to their room . . . where had that trail broken off? On which turn, at what particular point had that which he held slipped so irretrievably from his grasp?

He poured some more whisky into his glass though it wasn't yet empty. He found it a little odd that last night, too, he'd been drinking; but then he was high up in the clouds. When the air-hostess had announced that they were crossing the channel, he'd gazed down through the aeroplane window. He hadn't seen much; neither sea nor lighthouse—just darkness flowing from darkness—and, then, nothing at all. As he peered into the gloom, it occurred to him that the channel he could not discern below in fact lay somewhere within him . . . stretching from one of his lives to the next, and he'd eternally be crossing it; going this way and then that, belonging nowhere, neither coming from nor reaching anywhere . . . .

'Where's Bindu?'

He looked up startled. He did not know how long she'd been standing there. 'She's outside; in the garden,' he said. 'She is feeding the rabbits.'

She stood a little away from him, below the banister. She had put on a long maxi after her shower . . . . Hair loose, her face was washed and sparkling, the shower having cleansed its agitation. She looked at his glass on the table.

'There is ice, too, if you'd like some,' she said.

'No, thank you, I've taken some soda. Should I pour one for you?'

She shook her head; which could have meant anything. He knew she liked a cool drink after a warm bath. The years had done nothing to help him forget her habits; in fact, they formed the bridge by means of which they could return to a familiar world. He went into the kitchen and fetched a glass for her. He put some ice in it. While he was mixing the drink he heard her voice: 'That's enough.'

It was a voice washed of colour, tinged neither with affection nor with anger—calm and dispassionate. She had moved from the stairs and come up to the chair.

'Won't you sit down?' he asked, a little worried.

She picked up her glass and sat down on the stool near the TV, away from the table lamp, where only a thin sliver of light reached her.

For some time, neither of them spoke. Then the woman said, 'How is every one at home?'

'They're well . . . they've sent these things for you.'

'I know.' The woman's voice was edged with weariness. 'Why do you trouble the poor people? You drag these things here and they lie around uselessly.'

'That's all they can do,' he said. 'You haven't been there for years; they miss you.'

'Is there any point in going there now?' She took a deep draught from her glass. 'I have no relationship with them now.'

'Well, you could come with the child at least. She's never seen India.'

After a short silence, she said softly, 'She will be fourteen next year . . . legally she can go wherever she wants to after that.'

'I'm not talking of the legality; you know she won't go anywhere without you.'

The woman gazed at the man through the liquid depths of her glass. 'If I had my way, I'd never send her there!'

'But why is that?'

She laughed softly. 'Don't you think she's had enough of India between the two of us?'

He just sat there. After a while, the kitchen door opened and the girl entered. She looked at them silently and then walked to the staircase; to the telephone.

'Who are you ringing?' asked the woman.

The girl said nothing. She dialled the number. The man got up and looked at her. 'Will you have some more?'

'No . . . .' She shook her head. The man began to fill his glass slowly.

'Do you drink a lot?' asked the woman.

'No . . . .' The man shook his head. 'It tends to get a bit much when I travel.'

'I had thought you would have settled down with someone by now.'

'Why?' He gave the woman a look. 'What gave you that idea?'

The woman fixed expressionless eyes on him. 'Why, what happened to that girl? Doesn't she live with you?'

No agitation coloured the woman's voice, nor did it hold even a shadow of accusation . . . as though two individuals were discussing, years later, an incident that had, in one jerk, flung them on separate shores . . . .

'I live alone . . . . with *Amma*,' he said.

The woman looked at him. 'Why, what went wrong?'

'Nothing . . . maybe I'm not fit to live with.' His voice became unusually low, as though he were disclosing a secret ailment.

'Does it surprise you? But there are such people . . . .'

He wanted to say more; about love and fidelity, about belief and betrayal; an important truth, compounded of so many lies, that strikes like lightning in the haze induced by whisky, and the next moment is lost in the darkness and mist. Maybe the girl was waiting for just this minute; she left the phone and came up to the man. She looked once at her mother who sat half-hidden in the obscure corner behind the table lamp. And the man? He was a liquid blur behind his glass.

'Papa!' The girl held a slip of paper in her hand. 'This is the name of the hotel; the taxi will reach you there in ten minutes.'

He pulled the girl close and put the piece of paper in his pocket. The three sat quietly for a while, as, years ago, people congregated silently before starting out on a journey. Stars had come up outside and the old willow, the hedges and the rabbit enclosure had crept up close together in the still-yellow light.

He put his glass on the table, kissed the girl gently and picked up his suitcase. When the girl opened the door, he lingered for an instant on the threshold. 'Well, I'd better go now,' he said. It was difficult to tell who he said this to but no sound came from where she sat. The silence there was as thick as the darkness into which he was stepping.

THE FUNERAL PROCESSION
Shrikant Verma

There was room for just one cot inside. 'Has she got family?' The
constable emerged from the cramped quarter and put the question
to the crowd gathered outside. Seeing that he got no reply, he
mumbled, 'After all, we'll have to make arrangements to get her
removed from here!'

'Was she a Hindu or a Muslim?'

'She was a whore.' The speaker was a youth who stood leaning
back on his bicycle.

'I'm aware of that,' retorted the constable sternly.

'If you ask me, you ought to hand her over to the missionaries,'
suggested somebody else, offering a bundle of bidis to the
policeman.

'Is it true that the corpse has been lying around since yesterday?
What if it starts rotting? Constable Sahib, please make sure it's
disposed of quickly!'

Blowing out bidi smoke from his nostrils, the policeman said
'Well, to begin with, we'll have to find out if she's got people. We'll
have to report the matter at the police station too, because, if there's
anything shady about this, the bastards will pin it all on me! After
all, they expect us to have some idea of what we're doing.' He
puffed at the bidi, lost in thought. Groups of people silently stood
by. Some moved away, talking in whispers.

A bunch of shacks and living quarters of modest dimensions
stood at some distance. The uncemented road had acquired a
reddish hue from the gravel that the wind blew about throughout
the day, giving the settlement an air of desolation.

Imarti was the only woman to have lived there in the last couple
of years. She did not leave despite all the inconveniences she was
compelled to put up with. The inhabitants of the place had accepted her now. Indeed, there was no way they could show their
hostility. Of course, they could refuse to talk to her, but no oppor-

tunity for that presented itself anyway, except for the times when she dolled up to stand near the paan shop.

Nor did Imarti waste much time buying meat curry every evening at the Sindh Hindu Hotel, where the loudspeaker blared film songs from morning till midnight. Perhaps she knew, from experience, that people who frequented the place were louts who could not even pay for what they bought. She loathed such people. She had paid a youngster to inscribe on her wall, in well-formed, coloured letters, the words: 'Credit cuts through love.'

Imarti Bai was a whore with a difference. When she died the paan seller said she was a woman of few words. She was choosy about her customers, too, and in her last days entertained only the select. She wasn't the type most men would fancy, anyway. In the words of the paan seller, 'She neither sang nor wiggled her hips; men don't just want a body. It's different each time.' If any one should disagree—after all, men didn't visit her to enjoy a concert, they did want her body—he would be quick to retort, 'But you need a supple body, don't you? She had no coquettish tricks up her sleeve. A downright whore, that's what she was!'

He reiterated this as he folded the paan. 'I knew it would come to this! "Imarti Bai, get yourself treated," I said, "there is still hope for you." But the wretched woman preferred to pass on disease while she lived! Now she's dead and there's no one to pick up her body . . . you may not agree, but she was a whore through and through! I know everything about her.' He called out to the constable as he flicked *kattha* on the paan leaf and folded it deftly: 'Constable Sahib, get rid of the corpse soon—it's disease-ridden!'

The constable, meanwhile, was blowing into a glass of hot tea. He turned around at this, perhaps intending to say something. Just then, however, the municipal buffalo-cart that was used for transporting garbage turned into the lane. The constable gulped down his tea, and, handing the glass back to the lad from the teashop, moved forward eagerly towards the cart. 'What's your name, fellow?' he asked.

'Bansilal,' he said, climbing down from the cart.

'Where are you bound?'

'I'm on duty,' he replied casually. He didn't stand in any awe of policemen. If it hadn't been for the crowd he would not even have stopped there. He would have gone past, singing as usual. It had become a ritual of sorts with him to burst into song whenever he passed that way, whether he spotted Imarti Bai outside or not.

The policeman gave him a withering look. 'Well, listen to me, Bansilal; you'll have to forget about your duty for now, do you understand? You have to go to the cremation ground.'

'Why, who's dead?' asked Bansilal in surprise, tucking his stick away into the cart.

'Imarti Bai!' called out someone from the crowd.

'What was that?' He couldn't believe his ears. 'What did you say?'

'Remove the body from here and be quick about it, is that clear? I'm leaving now; I have to hand in a report at the police station.' The police constable patted Bansilal's shoulder conspiratorially. He entered something into a grubby notebook he'd produced from his pocket, and went on his way.

Bansilal had halted the cart at the edge of the road. 'All right, then, I'll take a look inside!' he said, pushing past the throng of people into the tiny room. He was accompanied by others, who, so far, had been hesitant to go inside.

The corpse lay on the bed. Nobody had bothered to cover it with a sheet. It was the first time Bansilal had entered the room, and he felt a pang as he did so. He had often seen Imarti. He was sure he'd be able to visit her one of these days. An image of the milk and rose body, still taut at the end of the long journey, flashed through his mind.

He had never saved up enough to go there, though. He was aware that Imarti entertained only choice customers; her rates were high and she would not come down. And what if she did? He was the last person she would look at. He was no stranger to the fact that he was ugly; his short, squat figure marking him out as a target for derision and pity. When confronted by the sniggers he invariably provoked, he could do nothing but swallow his anger and move on. Donning a white kurta and dhoti of fine material, he strolled over to the cinema house regularly in the evenings. The film tunes he played on his flute attracted a swarm of youngsters. It was thanks to this flute that he had developed quite a following.

Imarti's face was repulsive with the lips slightly parted. Her sari had slipped, exposing a breast, and her thigh was uncovered too. He felt a little sad seeing her in that condition and realized that he would have to hurry up with the job of removing the body.

Preoccupied with these thoughts, he moved forward and draped the sari over the corpse.

It was unnecessary to carry the bed outside. 'Will somebody give me a hand?' he asked, taking hold of the corpse by the legs. One man supported the neck and another the back. The corpse was carried outside. 'Give me five minutes,' he said eagerly. 'I'll give the cart a wash.' It wasn't as if he had never transported a corpse before. Yet, for the first time, he found the idea of laying it down in a dirty vehicle revolting.

Tapping the buffalo's back gently with his stick, he moved the cart under the tap and began to wash it with obvious enjoyment. Splashing water on to the cart with his hands, he then scrubbed it hard with a grimy rag. He jumped up once onto the buffalo's back to get a better view of the cart, and seemed to approve of what he saw. 'A little bit more . . . ,' he muttered to himself, and, climbing down, got back to work.

About a score of people were standing clustered round the body. He drove the cart recklessly towards them. 'Move aside, will you? Just give me some room!' he panted, descending, and then collected himself and shouted, 'Give me a hand with the corpse, please!' People moved forward to lift up the corpse 'Take it easy now . . . watch it!'

He jumped lightly up on to the cart and began to make room for the body. However, the space was not wide enough for the corpse to be laid down. He felt a little agitated and was vexed with the municipality. How could you expect to carry even a child's body in such a small cart?

'No, not that way . . . put her down like this.' A couple of people helped him settle the corpse into a half-reclining position. Untying his neckcloth, he made it into a pillow for the corpse's head. This gave him some satisfaction. Still standing on the cart, he ran a cursory glance over the crowd. He didn't quite know why he felt a notch higher than them. Not giving any one the time to talk to him, he whisked the cart forward and then sat down with relief.

A little further down the road, he turned around and noticed that the crowd had thinned considerably. A man had stepped forward to bolt the door to Imarti's quarters. He drove the cart faster and brought it to a halt at the turning. He got down from the cart and glanced around. The body still lay there, half-reclining.

With the movement of the cart the clothes had slipped away again, and, now, the body lay there, almost nude. He fixed a look on it and then turned away, embarrassed. With a deft movement, he draped the clothes over it again and moved in the direction of the paan shop.

The seven rupees he had saved up from his wages were intact in his pocket. For days he'd had a mental list of the things he planned to buy with them. Taking out the money from his pocket, he went up to the paan shop and said, 'Can you give me some change please?' The paan seller smirked at him, 'I don't have so much change.'

Pretending not to hear him, Bansi said, 'Hurry up please! It's getting to be time.'

He watched the paan seller take out a bag full of coins and count them. He felt somewhat encouraged when he'd got the little pouch full of coins and he sat up eagerly. As he drove past he could see the paan seller and some others jeering at him, to say nothing of the crude gestures the paan seller was making with the little stick he used for applying *kattha* to the paan. Showering silent curses on them, he brought the stick down hard on the buffalo's back.

Getting out of that settlement was a relief, though he perspired in the hot sun after such an effort. Signs of life had begun to be visible on the road. Some of the shops were open too. He turned around once to check up on the corpse. Every thing was fine except that the pillow had slipped a little. He stopped the cart and settled it back into place.

He thought the corpse moved a little under his touch and a spark flared up in him. The idea of touching her live body sent little currents shooting through him and his pulse quickened. Now he was back in his place again, building up a fantasy about that body in a sari. He had often seen her standing at the door wearing vibrant saris. Rani Roopmati. He always had the feeling that she stood there waiting for somebody and his heart beat faster when he walked into the lane and past her door. He would have a strong urge to look at her but could never bring himself to meet her eyes. Head lowered in embarrassment, he'd move on—on his way. When he'd look back at her from a distance, he'd find her still standing there; Rani Roopmati. He had woven an intangible relationship between that figure standing in the doorway and his own as he passed it. He would certainly go to her one day. He fumbled for the pouch in his lap and caressed it lovingly. Drawing out a handful of coins from it, he looked around him and then flung them high into the air. People sitting in shops and walking on the footpath started at the jingle of coins raining down. A throng of urchins and beggars jumped towards them. He stopped the cart and gazed at the crowd falling on the coins. Seeing that the road was now clear of coins, he produced another handful from the pouch and threw them up in to the air, crying out in a thick voice, '*Ram nam sat hai! Sabki yahi gat hai!*' The people collecting the coins mechanically repeated the words.

As he flicked the beast's back enthusiastically with his stick, the cart raced forward, bringing, in tow, the mass of people hungry for coins. At the next turn he halted the madly careening vehicle abruptly, and shouted once more, '*Ram nam sat hai! Sabki yahi gat hai!*' He had got quite a following by now; people were swarming around the cart, holding on to it, giving the odd impression that they bore a coffin.

A beggar, who happened to be walking near him, shouted over the din, 'Sethji, how about some music?'

Giving way to the turmoil within, he had shut his eyes. The beggar repeated his suggestion: 'Should I summon a band?'

'Yes.' This time he aimed the coins to the left of the road and the crowd flowed after them like a stream. In the meantime, another beggar had come up, laden with flowers and wreaths. The cart drew to a standstill. Bansi climbed down and strewed the flowers on the corpse.

'Who was it?' A piece of conversation floated up to him from the footpath.

'Imarti Bai.' As he laid down a wreath, his hand quivered with joy.

'Imarti Bai! Why, who was she?'

'A whore!'

Anger flashed through his eyes. 'She was a famous prostitute!' He looked at them with pride.

The band had arrived by then. 'Shall we begin, Sethji?'

'Yes, go ahead.'

He jumped up on to the cart as the music rose in the air, the strident notes attracting a bigger gathering. He took out some more coins from the bag and flung them on the road in a frenzy.

'*Ram nam sat hai! Sabki yahi gat hai!*'

It would be quite a job handling the enormous crowd, but he was confident he'd be able to do so. He had a fleeting desire to alter the direction of the funeral march and head straight back to Imarti's door. A flutter went through his heart, but he speeded up the cart, not allowing the flutter to surface. The sun had grown more intense. He would have to hurry with the rituals attending the death. He felt a pang at the thought that all would be over soon; if only this could go on and on!

He lifted his eyes and noticed that women, varying in age, had emerged on the terraces of the houses lining the road. He, rather than the crowd or the band, seemed to be the object of their attention. He looked at them unflinchingly, trying to make out what they said. He caught a few words over the noise of the music. 'Oh it's just Bansi, the mehtar!' He felt a rush of anger at the word 'mehtar' and he glared back at them.

This word was the proverbial Achilles' heel for him. He kept cleaner than many other people and he had advised youths belonging to his caste not to remove refuse should anyone call them a mehtar. He was deeply injured that these women had used that disagreeable name for him. He snapped at the beggar keeping pace with him to get the music played louder.

Not many coins were left in the pouch, he discovered, with consternation, as he fumbled in it. He should now be sagacious in their use. Instead of throwing coins on the road, he stood up on the tin edge of the cart. *'Ram nam sat hai!'*

The cremation site was situated outside the town, on the other side of the river. The bridge was visible in the distance.

He picked up some coins, and, using all his force, flung them hard so that they scattered everywhere. He watched elatedly as the bewildered crowd dispersed, following the direction of the coins.

He stopped the cart at the bridge. He handed the pouch with the rest of the money to a beggar and said peremptorily, 'Take them.'

The music stopped and the crowd of urchins turned back. A few stray passers-by were all that remained. He heard one of them say, 'I tell you, she moved!'

'What moved?' He leapt forward eagerly.

'Your corpse.'

Had it really moved? He had heard stories in which corpses had come alive; in fact, they sometimes even sat up on the funeral pyre.

He believed that life returns to the dead, though he could not have explained how it happened. Yet he knew doctors agreed that one should make absolutely sure before cremating a corpse.

He went round and bent over the corpse. It had certainly shifted a little from its place. His hand trembled in joyful disbelief. He pulled out the corpse's hand from under the sheet and felt the pulse. It was true, he could feel something beating very strongly. The body, however, was cold, and, when he passed his hand in front of the nose, no breath stirred upon it. What, then, was that beating? When he placed his hand on his own chest, he discovered its source—his heart was thudding madly, as though it were afflicted with an ailment.

Flicking his stick he got the cart rolling forward again, over the bridge. An expanse of water spread away on both sides to the shores where the sun glinted on little hillocks of sand. Having left the crowd far behind, he was all by himself now. Not a soul was in sight. The trundling of the cart's wheels was all that he could hear.

Over the bridge and down an incline; he entered the cremation ground and realized that it was quite deserted. The stench of a burning body assailed his nose. He stopped the cart with extreme caution right in front of the caretaker's house.

'Who is it?' asked the caretaker, opening his register.

'I've to cremate somebody.'

'Name?'

'Imarti Bai.'

'Age?'

'Thirty-two,' he said at once.

'Husband's name?' The caretaker glanced up at him.

Hesitating, just for a second, he looked around, as though to make sure no one was listening, then said, abruptly, 'Bansilal Balmiki.' He reached out a hand and put down his signature.

Outside, once more, he unloaded the corpse carefully from the cart. He draped the sari over it, taking care to see that it was completely covered. Then he picked up the spade and began to clear the ground where the funeral pyre would be built.

THE COLOUR BLUE
Vijay Chauhan

An emaciated old body. Hollow cheeks. A murky film of moisture covers listless brown eyes sunk deep in their sockets, giving them a strangely stony look. His overgrown hair is matted and quite grey. Pants that obviously haven't been washed in ages. Worn-out shoes with no laces. A faded blue blazer, ancient and threadbare. It is patched in a couple of places and a single button precariously holds the two sides together. A leather satchel in a battered condition.

A deep melancholy steals over me whenever I see this man. I'm not sure what it is that saddens me—is it the sight of him or of the blue of his blazer, now faded and quite lacklustre?

I love the colour blue. When I was a child I made all my pictures in blue. I would lie on my cot in the evening and gaze at the blue sky for hours. I possessed a blue coat too; and it was my favourite. Now when I look at his coat, I feel a pang for that blue which is no more. The colours I loved once have all vanished. The sight of them doesn't make me happy either. The clear blue sky and the white clouds swinging from it no longer urge me to break into song.

I remember a time, perhaps very long ago, when, wind tangling in the trees, rivulets breaking the silence of the forest, clouds floating across the sky, the chirping birds—all of these would make me want to sing with abandon.

Today a strange desolation settles over me when I see his patched coat and his inanimate eyes.

One day I stopped him and asked, 'Where is it that you go every day? You are old now; you should stay at home.'

He stopped, but did not seem to understand what I had said.

'Is there anything I can do for you?'

'Well, there are many things I need done. But what is it that you can do?'

'I repair broken-down machines.'

'What kind of machines?'

'All kinds. Sewing machines. Gramophones. Electric fans. I can mend anything in the house that's not working.'

I gave him my address and asked him to come by.

He passed my house every morning but never came in. I called out to him one day. He came inside and asked, 'Is there anything I can do for you?' I brought out the gramophone and placed it in front of him.

He sat down on the steps, opened his leather satchel and asked, 'Well, what's wrong with this?'

'There's nothing the matter with it, yet, but I'd like you to clean it for me anyway, and oil all the parts too.'

He opened the satchel and looked at me without a word.

'Why, what's wrong?' I asked.

'There's nothing in my bag.' Having said this, he closed the bag and looked like he wanted to go.

'If I get you some oil and a rag, will you clean this for me?'

He sat down on the veranda steps again. I got him a rag and some oil. He began to clean the gramophone. He asked me for a screwdriver. He opened all the screws and took the machine apart. He oiled all the parts and then said, 'Keep all these away carefully for the time being. I'll finish the work tomorrow.'

I did what he told me to. But he did not return for several days. One day I hailed him again.

He came to the veranda and asked, 'Is there anything I can do for you?'

'A gramophone's been taken apart. It needs to be put together again.'

He sat down on the veranda steps. I put all the gramophone parts before him. He opened his empty leather bag and looked at me. I went inside and fetched him the screwdriver. After working with the screwdriver for a long time, he said, 'I can't do this.'

He fixed his listless brown eyes on me. They were obscured with tears, or so it seemed to me.

'It's not your fault if you can't mend this. Why do you take it to heart?'

He did not wipe his eyes. A dirty film of moisture still clouded them. 'I've forgotten how to repair things. But maybe I'll remember if I work at it long enough.'

He picked up the screwdriver and worked with it again.

'Keep this screwdiver in your bag. I'll put these parts away carefully. You can come and work at them every day.'

He put the screwdriver in his satchel and went away.

One day he was sitting in the veranda, working on the machine as usual, when a man came up to me and said, 'Why did you let this man come in? He doesn't know how to repair anything!'

Then he turned to the man in the blue coat and said, 'Come with me now. You've ruined the gramophone already.'

The man in the blue coat stretched his legs out. He was obviously reluctant to go.

'If you won't come willingly . . . .' The younger man grasped his hand and dragged him to his feet. He wrenched the screwdriver away from his clenched fist and put it near the gramophone. The man in the blue jacket was still unwilling to leave. The younger man lifted him up in his arms. The man in the blue coat caught hold of the other's shirt with one hand and pulled off his glasses with the other. 'Watch it! Make sure you don't break my glasses . . . .' Then the younger man said to me, 'Well, I'll go now. I'm taking him with me too.'

I could see that. I said, 'But why do you treat the poor fellow like that? He works here every day; how does he bother you?'

'I am his son!'

The glasses dangled from the father's hand but he still clung to his son's shirt with the other.

'Now don't you ever step out of the house again without telling me!'

'I will.'

'No, you won't. I'll take away your bag and your blue jacket.'

The father returned the glasses. He fumbled with the buttons on his son's shirt and muttered, 'Okay, I won't step out of the house again without telling you.'

The son put him down. The father picked up his bag and looked at me. The film of muddy moisture had covered his eyes again.

He went away with his son. I watched his blue coat fading far into the distance. A drifting patch of dismal sky, the sight of which no longer filled me with rapture.

THE HOMECOMING
Usha Priyamvada

Gajadhar *Babu* glanced at the luggage piled up in the room—two trunks, a basket, bucket . . . . 'What's in this box, Ganeshi?' he queried.

Ganeshi was rolling up the bedding. His voice simultaneously held pride, anguish and bashfulness. 'The wife has packed some *besan laddus* for you; she said you love them, and since we won't now get an opportunity to serve you often . . . .'

Though he was happy about going home, Gajadhar *Babu*, nevertheless, experienced a stab of regret for the simple warmth and respectability of a familiar world; his links with which were being severed.

'Do think of us sometimes!' said Ganeshi, making fast a rope round the bedding.

'You must write to me if you need anything, Ganeshi! And do keep to your plan for your daughter's wedding in December.'

Ganeshi wiped his eyes with his neckcloth. 'I've been depending on your help for the wedding. Your presence would have been so reassuring!' Gajadhar *Babu* was ready to leave. The railway quarter he had occupied for years looked shabby, stripped of his possessions. Acquaintances had dug up and taken away his plants, too, and little mounds of earth were left piled up here and there. However, with the prospect of living with his family before him, anguish rose within him like a feeble wave and then died away.

Gajadhar *Babu* was rapturous. He had retired after thirty-five years of service, the major part of which he'd spent alone. This was the time he had fantasized about in those lonely years—when he would go home. This hope had given him the strength to cope with the burden of his isolation. He would have been called successful in the eyes of the world. He'd built his own house in the city; married off his elder son, Amar, and his daughter, Kanti, while two others were studying in senior classes at school. Gajadhar *Babu*'s job was such that he had often to be stationed in small suburbs, his family had always lived in the city so that his children's education may continue undisturbed.

Being affectionate by nature, he deserved similar affection himself. When he'd come home from work, he would engage his children in lively conversation and keep his wife entertained with jokes. A deep solitude settled on his life when they left. He never spent his free time at home. Though he was not a particularly romantic sort of person, he missed his wife's warmth. She did not allow the afternoon heat to get her down and baked hot rotis for him when he came home from work. She insisted, lovingly, that he have another helping when he'd finished. Somehow, she always heard his footsteps when he came home exhausted and appeared at the kitchen door, her shy eyes lighting up in a smile. These were the little details of their life together that Gajadhar *Babu* yearned for in his loneliness and the contemplation of which made him pensive. Now, however, the opportunity had presented itself at last when he was free to breathe in that warmth again.

Gajadhar *Babu* took off his cap and placed it on the bed.Then he undid his shoes and slid them under the bed, listening to the peals of laughter issuing from the house. It was Sunday and his children were at breakfast together. A contented smile still played on Gajadhar *Babu*'s shrivelled-up face when he walked into the room without coughing as usual. He was just in time to see Narendra dancing, mimicking last night's film, while Basanti doubled up with laughter. Amar's wife was laughing uncontrollably, too, quite unaware that her sari had slipped off her head. Narendra sat down with a thump the minute he saw Gajadhar *Babu* and hurriedly raised his cup of tea to his lips. His daughter-in-law became self-conscious, too, and quickly covered her head, only Basanti still shook in an effort to stifle her mirth.

Gajadhar *Babu* looked at them with a smile. 'Why, what kind of mime was that , Narendra?'

'Oh, nothing at all, *Babuji!*' said Narendra, embarrassed. Gajadhar *Babu* was a little annoyed at the abrupt end to the merriment he had hoped to participate in, but he seemed to have inhibited everybody. He sat down and asked, 'Basanti, will you pour me some tea? Is your mother still praying?'

Basanti's glance travelled to her mother's room. 'I think she's coming.' She began to strain the tea in a cup for him. His daughter-in-law had been the first to go away quietly, and, now, Narendra too drained his cup and stood up. Only Basanti was left sitting there, out of regard for her father. Gajadhar *Babu* sipped his tea and commented, 'Child, there's no sugar in this!'

'Here, give it to me; I'll put in some,' said Basanti.

'No, leave it for the time being. I'll have some tea with your mother.'

His wife emerged a little later, holding a pot of holy water, and, mumbling an indistinct prayer, she poured it on the tulsi plant in the yard. Basanti stood up to leave as soon as she saw her mother. 'Oh, they've left you sitting here alone! Where have they gone?' asked his wife as soon as she saw Gajadhar *Babu*.

Gajadhar *Babu* felt a twinge of pain. He said, 'I expect they're all busy with their own things; they're only children after all!'

His wife settled down in the kitchen, screwing up her nose at the pile of dirty dishes. 'All the dishes are dirty,' she complained. 'There is no place for religion in this house. Am I expected to start working in the kitchen the minute I finish praying?' She called out to the servant, and, seeing that she got no reply, she said shrilly, '*Bahu* must have sent him to the market!' Then she sighed and lapsed into silence.

Gajadhar *Babu* was waiting for his breakfast. Suddenly he thought of Ganeshi. He had fried hot puris for Gajadhar *Babu* in the morning even before the passenger train got in; before Gajadhar *Babu* was up and dressed. He made delicious tea as well; the glass filled to the brim, two-and-a-half spoons of sugar and thick cream. It was possible to conceive of the passenger train arriving late at Ranipur, but difficult to imagine Ganeshi delaying his tea; why, he'd never had to tell him off for anything!

His wife's petulant voice broke into his reverie. What she said was, 'I spend the whole day sorting out one mess or another. Look at the grey hair I've got trying to keep this household together. Nobody lifts a finger to help me.'

'Why, how does *Bahu* spend her time?' asked Gajadhar *Babu*.

'Oh, she just lazes about. Basanti, of course, has to attend college.'

Gajadhar *Babu* became agitated enough to call out to Basanti. When she emerged from her sister-in-law's room, he told her, 'Basanti, from tonight, you'll be cooking the dinner. Your sister-in-law will prepare the morning meal.'

Basanti pulled a long face and said, 'But, *Babuji*, I need some time to study too.'

Gajadhar *Babu* explained the situation to her lovingly. 'You can study in the morning. Your mother is old now; she is no more as energetic as she used to be. Both you and your sister-in-law should give her a hand.'

Basanti preferred to say nothing. When she had gone her mother said softly, 'Her studies are just an excuse. She's not really interested in books at all, and I'm not surprised! As if she gets any time away from Sheela. There are young boys in that house; I've told her many times that she shouldn't spend all her time there, but who listens?'

Gajadhar *Babu* retired to the living-room after breakfast. It was a small house and had been arranged in such a fashion as to leave no room in it for him. The chairs in the living-room had been pushed against the wall, as though to make room for a guest, and Gajadhar *Babu*'s narrow bed had been placed in the middle. When he lay down in that room, he sometimes, quite involuntarily, began to see the uncertainty of his situation in the house. It reminded him of trains that arrived at a station, halted for a while and then moved away to another destination.

He had been accommodated in the living-room because there was no other place for him. It was true that his wife had a small room to herself, but it was hemmed in by jars of pickle, dal, canisters of rice and tins of ghee. Old quilts had been piled up on another side, rolled up in coarse matting and secured with rope. Enormous metal trunks, containing the family's woollens, were lined up next to the quilts. This was not all; a clothesline had been stretched across the middle of the room, on which Basanti carelessly slung her clothes. He tried his best to avoid going into that room.

Amar and his wife used the other room. The living-room was right in front. Before Gajadhar *Babu* arrived, that room had held a set of three cane chairs gifted by his daughter-in-law's people. The daughter-in-law had embroidered the blue cushions herself.

Gajadhar *Babu*'s wife came into the living-room with her mat one day and lay down on it, which meant that she had a serious grievance to register. Gajadhar *Babu* commented that he had noticed the way things were going in the house. He tried to drop a gentle hint that expenses should be minimized, keeping in mind their reduced income.

for him to be drawn to those meetings. His happiness crossed all limits, however, the day his name was added on to the list of speakers and was called out on the loudspeaker: 'Now, the prime spokesman of the Muslims in our district, *Janab* Wasiullah Khan Sahib, will present his thoughts before you.'

And, for the first time, Wasiullah's name became *Janab* Wasiullah Khan Sahib. This unexpected honour left a profound impression on Wasiullah who stood on the stage and delivered a grand speech. He especially highlighted the problems faced by minorities, and drew the attention of the government representatives to them. Then he sang the praises of the party in question and declared it to be the sole well-wisher of the Muslims. There was a burst of applause from the stage at this, and the public had to clap loudly in response, too. Wasiullah could hardly contain his pride! He glowed!

All the leaders made a special effort to see Wasiullah after the meeting and everybody ended up having tea at his place. As it happened, the candidate fighting the election was a Muslim, and he had become Wasiullah's fan. He declared Wasiullah to be the regional representative of the minorities. Thus, *Janab* Wasiullah metamorphosed, in a single day, from an ordinary mortal into a very special person.

Wasiullah approved of this change. He came to command a heightened respect in the neighbourhood and began to be known as the right-hand man of Majharul Haq Sahib. Haq Sahib had become a minister after his victory in the elections. Wasiullah Khan was away from home often now, on the pretext of meeting Haq Sahib and, wherever possible, bragged about himself too. Till now, however, he hadn't been of help to anyone. He was making quite an impact on people, though. Most people, particularly the ones who couldn't read or write, looked up to him; but there were some who thought him nothing but a fool. They teased him, calling him Haq Sahib's flunkey. All this had no effect on Wasiullah, though. Dressed in a pyjama and kurta made from rough handwoven cloth, a Gandhi cap completing his attire, he would emerge, slapping his rubber slippers uninhibitedly. If anyone poked fun at him, he arrived at the conclusion that they must be Haq Sahib's rivals. In this way his politicking picked up speed.

Now he completely wound up the work he had previously been engaged in, and began to practise politics full-time. His involve-

He was a little taken aback when his wife retorted sharply, 'What am I to cut down on? We have no unreasonable expenses. I've wasted my youth trying to make ends meet; I've never even had the chance to wear the kind of clothes I wanted!'

Gajadhar *Babu* shot a wounded look at her. He was aware of his stringent circumstances. It was to be expected that his wife would feel the pinch, but it was the sheer absence of sympathy from her that stung him to the quick. Perhaps he would have been less hurt if she'd discussed the problem with him and arrived at a solution. She, however, only complained as though he were solely responsible for the woes of the family.

'What don't you have, Amar *ki* ma?' he said with genuine emotion. 'Children, a daughter-in-law . . . . after all it's not just money that makes one rich!' This was an expression of his innermost feelings, but his wife could not be expected to understand.

'Yes, isn't it a pleasure to have *Bahu* around? She's cooking today, let's see what she comes up with!' His wife dozed off.

Gajadhar *Babu* was left staring at her. Was this the same woman whose soft smile and gentle touch he had yearned for in his loneliness? The beautiful woman he had once known seemed to have got lost along the way, and the one who had replaced her was a total stranger . . . . He looked at his sleeping wife; her ponderous frame appeared ugly and her face devoid of any attraction. He gazed dispassionately at her for a long time and then lay down, fixing his eyes on the ceiling.

The noise of something falling woke his wife, who sat up hurriedly. 'There, the cat's upset something!' she exclaimed and ran into the kitchen. She was in a huff when she returned a little later. 'Look what *Bahu* has done! She left the kitchen door ajar and now the cat's upset the pot of dal. Nobody has eaten yet; what am I supposed to feed them now?' She paused for breath and continued, 'She's finished the whole tin of ghee frying four parathas and one vegetable. The heartless creature has no qualms about using up all the rations! I told you no one else could be trusted in the kitchen!'

Gajadhar *Babu* felt he'd go mad if his wife said anything more. He pursed his lips and turned his back on her.

Basanti had deliberately cooked an unpalatable meal. It was difficult to swallow even a mouthful. Gajadhar *Babu* ate in stoic silence, but Narendra pushed away his thali, saying, 'I can't eat such food!'

Basanti flared up too. 'Don't eat it then. Nobody's forcing you!'

'Who asked you to cook, anyway?' shouted Narendra.

'*Babuji* did.'

'I should have guessed as much. *Babuji*'s got nothing better to do!'

Amma made Basanti leave the table and placated Narendra. She even cooked something and fed him herself.

Later, Gajadhar *Babu* remarked to his wife, 'She's a grown-up girl now, but she can't cook a decent meal!'

'Oh, it's not that she can't cook; she just doesn't want to!' replied his wife.

The next evening *Amma* was in the kitchen when Basanti dressed and came out.

Gajadhar *Babu* called out to her from the living-room, 'Where are you going?'

'I'm just going to Sheela's.'

'No, you're not! It's a much better idea to go inside and study.' Gajadhar *Babu*'s tone was harsh. Basanti went inside after a moment of indecision.

When Gajadhar *Babu* returned from his walk that evening, his wife asked him, 'What did you say to Basanti? She's been moping the whole evening. She hasn't eaten either!'

Gajadhar *Babu* was annoyed. He preferred not to reply to his wife, but made a silent resolve to arrange for Basanti's wedding soon. After that day Basanti avoided meeting her father. If she needed to go out she did so through the back door. When Gajadhar *Babu* asked his wife why she did that, he got the reply, 'She's in a huff.' Gajadhar *Babu* found his annoyance increasing. What a temper his daughter had! Just because he'd asked her not to go out she wouldn't talk to him! Then his wife informed him that Amar was contemplating the idea of moving out.

'Why?' asked Gajadhar *Babu*, astonished.

His wife did not give him a clear answer. Amar and his wife had many grievances. Gajadhar *Babu* was always in the living-room; where were they to entertain visitors? His father still considered Amar a child, and ticked him off whether or not the occasion demanded. His wife was compelled to work in the kitchen and her mother-in-law made fun of her clumsiness.

'Did he ever think of moving out before I came?' asked Gajadhar *Babu*.

His wife shook her head. Amar had been the master of the house then. His friends had been regular visitors, and Basanti had enjoyed these get-togethers too. His wife had never been put to any inconvenience either.

Gajadhar *Babu* said very softly, 'Tell Amar there's no need for such haste.'

When he returned from his walk the next morning, Gajadhar *Babu* found that his bed had been removed from the living-room. On the verge of enquiring, he remembered something and remained silent. He peeped into his wife's room and discovered that his bed had been laid out in the midst of the jars and quilts. He took off his coat and looked for a place on the wall to hang it. Then he folded it and made some room for it on the clothesline. He lay down without eating. His body was old. Though he still took regular walks, he was tired by the time they ended.

Gajadhar *Babu* found himself thinking about his spacious railway quarter—an ordered life, the bustle of activity at the station when the passenger train steamed in, familiar faces and the music of trains clattering past on the tracks. Indeed, he got solace in his lonely nights from the sound of trains steaming past. Workers from Seth Ramjimal's mill often walked across for a friendly chat; they constituted his circle of friends. That life suddenly seemed a lost treasure. He felt cheated, not having got even a little of all he had wanted.

He lay in bed listening to the sounds percolating from the house; the tiff between the mother and daughter-in-law, the bucket filling under the open tap, utensils clinking in the kitchen, chirruping sparrows. He made up his mind never to interfere in domestic matters again. If there was no room in the house for the master's bed, he would lie where he was; if moved from there too, he'd go like a lamb. If his children had no time for him he would reconcile to living like a stranger in his own house . . . and, in fact, Gajadhar *Babu* did not meddle in the affairs of the house after that. When Narendra wanted money, he gave it without asking questions. He did not protest when Basanti stayed out of the house after dark. He was deeply saddened, however, by the fact that even his wife sensed no change in him. She remained a stranger to the burden of sacrifice that he bore in resolute silence. If anything, she was relieved at his aloofness. Sometimes she even voiced this feeling: 'The children have grown up now; you don't have to tell them what to do. We're doing our duty by educating them and seeing to it that they get married!'

Gajadhar *Babu* shot an injured look at his wife. He'd begun to feel he was just a source of money for his family. Wasn't it because of him that his wife put vermilion in the parting of her hair and got respect from society? And here she considered herself absolved of her duties towards him just because she served him two meals a day! The tins of ghee and sugar were all that mattered to her now. Gajadhar *Babu* was no more at the centre of her life, and he found himself losing enthusiasm in his daughter's wedding too. He remained an outsider in his home. His presence in the house was as incongruous as his bed was in the living-room. His happiness at being home had dissolved into deep disappointment.

But, at times, despite his resolve not to interfere, Gajadhar *Babu* could not prevent himself from doing so. His wife was complaining about the servant as usual: 'He's such a shirker! And it's not just that, he makes a profit on everything he buys for us. Then you should see him eat! He never wants to stop!' Gajadhar *Babu* was plagued by the feeling that expenses were soaring above his budget. When he heard his wife talk like that, he felt that the servant was a source of unnecessary expenditure. One of the three men at home could do the small jobs that needed to be done around the house. He fired the servant that very day.

When Amar got home from work and called the servant, his wife informed him, '*Babuji*'s got rid of him.'

'Why?'

'He says he was too expensive.'

The conversation was straightforward enough, but Gajadhar *Babu* did not like his daughter-in-law's tone of voice.

Overcome by dejection, Gajadhar *Babu* did not take his evening walk. He felt too lazy to even get up and switch on the light. That was how it happened that Narendra did not see him in the dark when he said to his mother, '*Amma*, why did *Babuji* fire the servant? Can't he find something else to do? And you didn't even try and stop him! If he thinks I'm going to lug the wheat on my bike to the mill, he's mistaken!'

'That's true, *Amma*! It's too much to have to sweep the house when I get back from college.' This time it was Basanti's voice.

'He's an old man . . . ,' murmured Amar. 'Why doesn't he keep his nose out of things?'

His mother retorted sarcastically, 'Yes, when he ran out of ideas he sent your wife into the kitchen. She finished off fifteen days' ration in five.' Before Amar could think of a reply she went into the kitchen. When she switched on the light in her room a short while later, she was startled to see Gajadhar *Babu* lying there, quietly, with his eyes shut. It was difficult to gauge his thoughts.

*

Gajadhar *Babu* entered the house waving a letter and called out to his wife. She emerged, wiping her wet hands. Without a preamble, he said, 'I've got a job in Seth Ramjimal's sugar mill. He had asked me before but I had refused. I've changed my mind now because there is no point in being idle . . . and, then, there'll be some more money too.' Then he said, very softly, as if he were making a feeble attempt to keep a dying fire alive, 'I'd thought I'd be free to live with my family at last, but I have to go the day after. Will you come with me?'

'I?' stuttered his wife. 'If I go with you, who's going to look after such a big establishment, and then a grown-up girl in the house . . . .'

Gajadhar *Babu* cut her short resignedly, 'That's all right, you stay here. I wasn't serious.' He lapsed into a deep silence.

Narendra tied up the bedding with great dexterity and hailed a rickshaw. Gajadhar *Babu*'s tin trunk and modest bedding was placed on it. Carrying the basket containing cookies for his breakfast, he boarded the rickshaw. He glanced round at his family and then looked away as the rickshaw jerked into motion.

Everybody came back inside when he had left.

Amar's wife asked him, 'You'll take me to the pictures today, won't you?'

Basanti jumped up with joy and said, 'What a good idea! I want to come too!'

Gajadhar *Babu*'s wife headed straight back to the kitchen. She kept the leftover cookies in a box which she put near the canisters in her room. Then she came out and said, 'Narendra, will you remove *Babuji*'s bed from the living-room? It's so cramped, there's no room in there to walk!'

THE FESTIVAL
Mehrunnisa Parvez

The brown cat had laid kittens inside the empty rice drum. They were tan-coloured and soft; a little like raw flesh. She sat sheltering them, growling whenever any body passed by. Shano stood on the wooden stairs, looking down.

Amma was looking out for Shano. Waking up in the morning was a torment for the children. Shano barely crawled out of bed before it was time to think about school.

With her turmeric yellow voile dupatta flying in the breeze, Shano had to cover the distance to school every morning. Life was hard; she was not excused from school, even today, when the brown cat had laid kittens.

Amma was lying in wait for her. 'There you are! Still hanging about on the stairs and the sun is already high in the sky! Won't you go to school today?'

Shano reluctantly climbed down the stairs and came into the kitchen when *Amma* scolded her. It was certainly easier to take the beating *Janabji* would invariably inflict on her if she wasn't hungry.

When she saw Shano, *Amma* served the stale food on a plate. The girl sat down on a worn straw mat and began to gulp down her food. 'It's early in the day yet, but the hut already looks like it's in flames!' *Amma* shouted on her way to the well.

The sun chose to rise each morning only over Kalo the barber's broken mud wall. His mother would say proudly, 'It was my mother who chased the sun up into the sky with her broom or it would still have been down here!'

The children of the locality were eager to find out why the sun didn't come first to their yard; why did it always rise over Kalo's broken mud wall?

The barber's daughter-in-law had been suffering after-birth pains since last night. She had given birth to her third son just the day before. *Amma* said only some people suffered after-birth pain.

The uterus moved around, looking for the baby; this was the reason for the pain.

Kalo's mother was distressed at the sight of her daughter-in-law in agony.

Amma asked Shano to take some roasted potatoes for Kalo's wife. 'Here you are . . . take care to give them discreetly to her, and make sure you stand at the foot side of the bed!' *Amma* admonished.

Amma was well-versed in indigenous medicine and the charms she gave to people were usually very effective. She had tried her medicines on Father, too, but they didn't help—for once—and he succumbed to asthma. *Aapa* sat on *Abba*'s broken cane chair, unravelling her old sweater.

According to *Aapa*, if you undid an old sweater, wound the wool into neat skeins and washed it, the wool became new again.

The strains of a lullaby drifted over from Kalo's yard—'*A rush swing dear, for the Queen Mother to swing on . . . .*'

Shano was strutting about, rocking her doll to sleep. The brown cat had strayed from the drum in search of food and a thin meowing issued from in there.

'*Amma*, it's the month of Ramzan now. Send for some lime; I'll whitewash the house.'

Amma preferred not to reply. She silently continued to pick grit from the rice. *Aapa* levelled an attentive look at her mother and bent over the skeins of wool again.

The sun had crept into the yard. The enormous iron front-door was quite dilapidated and hung to one side. The adjacent wall had collapsed in the last rains too. One half of the road was visible from the broken wall. It was from there that *Khala* was seen approaching. She carried a wicker basket in her hand. Everyone called her *Khala*-with-the-eggs. She had started selling eggs when her husband died.

'Oho! What hypocrites these rich people are! They poke fun at me just because I sell eggs for a living! What about Karim's fancy wife who became a schoolteacher as soon as her man died?' The words broke loose from *Khala*'s mouth as soon as she entered the room.

'Well, I don't blame her, sister! Her husband foisted three children on her and died. Is she going to tuck them away in a basket if she doesn't work to feed them?' *Amma* commented, picking up the grains of rice that had fallen on the floor.

Khala nodded in silent affirmation. Selling eggs from door to door, dressed in clothes that people distributed as zakat, she was a walking newspaper; she could tell you all about the locality. *Khala*, who was short in height, did not observe rules regarding fasting and prayer. Should anyone comment on this, she said, succinctly, '*Bhai*, I can't run my business without resorting to lies! And does it make sense for a liar to fast? Poor folks like me are compelled to fast every day anyway!'

Shano wiped her grimy hands on the curtain.

Amma scolded her, 'Haven't I told you not to use the curtain for a towel?'

'*Khala*, how many saris do you expect to get in Ramzan, this year?'

'Go on! Who wants to give zakat in these rough times? Though, do you remember Jiya, who came here with his children last year? He's promised to send me some clothes.'

Aapa's eyes strayed to *Khala*'s feet, which were covered with eczema, the black medicine on the rashes making them ghastlier.

'So long, then! I'll be on my way; I still have far to go.' *Khala* picked up her basket and prepared to leave.

A hush settled down once she had gone. *Amma* went inside with the rice she had cleaned. Shano stood in the sunshine shooing away crows perched on the wall.

Abba had died when Shano was just a year old. *Amma* made medicinal brews and sold them for a living. She was just a thin cage of bones now, and how irritable she had grown lately!

Jiya *Bhai* came last summer—he was distantly related to *Amma*. He'd only spent two days with them, but they seemed like two years. They had tried their best to hide their poverty from him, but it was difficult to conceal anything with Shano around. The girl had blurted out that, with their fields mortgaged to Guptaji, they had to buy grain in order to eat.

The two days seemed to have aged *Amma*. She had thrashed Shano in the backyard but that didn't help. After all, Jiya Bhai could see for himself, couldn't he? He had given a ten-rupee note to Shano when he left, and, later, *Amma* had beaten Shano again for accepting it. The frightened girl had spent the day hiding behind Kalo's broken wall.

The brown cat was lazing in the sunshine. The mosque was clearly visible; someone was up on the minaret, whitewashing it. The new house with the yard opening on to the road was being cleaned too. It wasn't long for Id.

She was sewing a patch on the blind. Shano came running inside, '*Aapa*, the Ramzan moon has been sighted! Everyone is talking about it!'

'Really, did you see it?'

'Yes, I stood near Kalo's broken wall and saw it; it was a thin slice of moon!'

'What's the matter? What are you shouting for?' asked *Amma* coming into the yard.

'*Amma*, the Ramzan moon has been sighted!'

Amma went pale; then she composed herself at once. 'It will be Id soon! These festivals keep coming back so quickly, don't they?'

Amma went back inside the room. Shano ran out again. She remembered the eager anticipation they had associated with Id before . . . now a hush settled on the house at a mention of the word.

Id had given Shano the excuse to repeat, like a parrot, that she wanted a *gharara* with dots on it, in pink satin.

Aapa sympathized with *Amma*'s dejection, though. *Amma* sat silently staring into the dark.

The days of fasting seemed as empty as they were long; there was no work about the house either. She loitered about the yard the whole day. The kittens, much bigger now, hid behind the door, meowing. Shano watched them throughout the day.

Much action was taking place in the houses nearby. White-washing was in progress; clothes were being stitched and vermicelli made. *Amma*'d had enough of festivals; they only annoyed her now. In her opinion, festivals came only to strip people naked before others.

The new house on the hill belonged to Ramzani. Once upon a time, Ramzani's widowed mother, Fatima, had lived in a dilapidated shack. She had sold meat for a living and that was how she brought up Ramzani. Ramzani, who had once been the boy who delivered meat to homes, was now one of the wealthy in the locality. There was a crowd of beggars at his door every Thursday and Friday. He distributed clothes on the twenty-seventh day of

Ramzan every year. Religious meetings, attended by a priest, were held at his place on a grand scale.

Amma was annoyed if anyone mentioned Ramzani. 'These are the signs of doom mentioned in the *Quran* . . . . People of humble origins will build solid houses and make lots of money, whereas those with ancestral money will become impoverished!' she proclaimed.

There was a crowd at Ramzani's door early on the twenty-seventh day of Ramzan. Beggars sat around asking strange questions.

Amma had sent for some lime at *Aapa*'s insistence, and now she was busy whitewashing the house, her dupatta drawn tightly round her. The house was in a mess, with droplets of lime everywhere. Shano was drawing lines in the lime that had dropped on the floor. There were just three days to go for Id; she counted on her fingers. Her desire for the dotted satin *gharara* was gaining strength. Her friends already had new clothes and wondered why she didn't have any yet. She nagged *Amma* all the time, 'After all, why haven't we got our new clothes? What's the delay?'

Amma was at her wits' end trying to explain that they were poor now. They wouldn't have new clothes for Id, or go visiting either. They would stay home and have everyone talk about them. The pallor of *Amma*'s face seemed more pronounced. And the lines on it conveyed a permanent irritability.

Khala had been round several times to check up on their new clothes. *Amma* evaded *Khala*'s questions, but grumbled later, 'Are new clothes necessary for Id? Why do people pester us? After all, we don't go digging out skeletons from their cupboards!'

Khala was in the crowd at Ramzani's . . . . Shano had come in with this bit of news. *Amma* wasn't at all pleased. 'Her man isn't cold in his grave yet, and she's joined the beggars! The shameless hussy only wears clothes she gets as zakat!'

'I'm not going to school tomorrow if I don't have new clothes!' Shano flung herself face down on the bed with this last warning.

What on earth was *Amma* doing in that room? She was making enough noise to wake the dead. Going up, close, *Aapa* saw that *Amma* had the trunk open and was taking out an old Banarsi sari, now quite moth-bitten. 'Look, I'll use this to stitch a *gharara* for Shano. Won't it look pretty?'

'Oh, but you couldn't cut a whole sari just to get one *gharara* out of it?'

'Uh! There's no life in it now anyway! The poor child is pining away for a new *gharara*!'

She noticed that *Amma*'s face had brightened up.

Amma had just settled down with the sari and a pair of scissors when Shano scampered in.

'*Amma*, there's a postman outside our house; he's brought a parcel!'

'Talk sense! Who'd send a parcel here? Are parcels arriving from the graveyard these days?'

Shano was on the verge of tears.

'Is any one home? Come and take your parcel!' It was the postman's voice.

'It's true, *Amma*; look, the postman's here!'

Amma went outside eagerly.

'Will you sign this? Or put a thumb imprint perhaps . . . ?' asked the postman.

Amma pressed her thumb down on the paper. They could not take their eyes off the big bundle; they stared at it in astonishment. Shano snatched it from her mother's hand and read the name on it.

'*Amma*, it's from Monghyr.'

She picked up the scissors, slit open the edges of the parcel and pulled out its contents. A length of flowered satin came into her hands. It was yellow. Shano did a little jig for joy.

'Who could have sent this from Monghyr?'

'*Amma*, don't you remember? Jiya Bhai lives in Monghyr, doesn't he?'

'Oh! So now we know who sent this!' *Amma* caressed the material. 'Give it here, I'll cut out a *gharara* at once—there aren't many days left for Id!'

It was a long time since *Amma* had pronounced the word 'Id' with some emphasis. Her face glowed with pleasure. It was good to see *Amma* happy; it took a load off *Aapa*'s chest.

Shano ran whooping with joy to fetch an old *gharara* on which the new one was to be modelled. *Amma* would show off the cloth to *Khala* when she visited them in the evening. *Khala* accepted zakat and, in doing so, had shed the mantle of respectability just as she had left off wearing a burqa when her husband died.

The gloom that had settled on the house seemed to have fled by way of the coal-tar road.

A peon from the court had brought in a notice of bankruptcy for *Amma*. The bearer of the note arrived in the afternoon, when all the doors were shut, for it was customary to shut the doors at meal and rest times. It was lucky nobody saw him or *Amma* would have been plagued by questions before the day was out.

So many questions about the future loomed threateningly in front of *Amma*. She was in a daze. Why had her face turned so white lately? She was faced with a horrifying and unbearable truth. She missed *Abba* today, but not as much as her dead son Shamim. For Shamim was her anchor once her husband died.

Kalo's mother had just come in with a broken tile on which she wanted to take some hot coals from *Amma*'s fire. The imprint of small wet feet in the yard belonged to Shano. *Amma* quietly lay on Shano's little cot, her eyes fixed on the black bamboo beams of the ceiling. Silence hung about the house, and memories of the past filled the hush. She wanted to reach out and grasp them, like she had caught butterflies when she was a child.

People bustled around, eager to catch a glimpse of the moon. Many points of debate had cropped up. The moon had not been spotted yet; would Id be celebrated on the thirtieth day of the moon?

Darkness had grown deeper. Shano sat hunched up over her book, repeating her lesson by the light of the lantern. In its glow, the blind cast criss-crossing shadows in the room.

Khala could be seen briskly approaching, carrying a bag in one hand. She made herself comfortable on the floor near Shano.

'The moon hasn't been seen yet, *Khala*, has it?'

'No, but Kalo says it's been seen in Pakistan. The wretched moon goes there first too!'

Shano leaped towards *Khala*'s bag, her knees curled up like a frog's. 'What's in this, *Khala*?'

'Wait a minute, will you? That's what I've come to show you . . . . I received a parcel today,' *Khala* said proudly.

'A parcel!' *Amma* had walked up.

'Oh, d'you remember, I told you, I was expecting some clothes from Jiya who lives in Monghyr? Well, he's sent me this material as zakat this year. I thought it might make a pretty dress for Shano . . . !' *Khala* explained as she opened her bag. She spread the material out in the sickly light of the lantern . . . it was the same yellow-flowered satin. *Amma* leaned back against the wall. Her shadow quivered in the uncertain glow of the lantern. Her yellow eyes were brimming over like a monsoon drain.

TRAFFIC JAM
Sanjeev

As though in response to the cracking of a whip, our hooves compelled us into progressively faster, more passionate, motion. Sweating, foaming at the mouth, we had metamorphosed into horses at the racecourse. Bending and skirting, wending and weaving, avoiding some and taking other roads, when we stopped our bicycles at the crossroad, the terror of the unquiet city had flared up. Our arms felt like they'd been scorched with live coals; we were burning like dead bodies and the gulmohar clouds were also red, like tattered corpses. Caught in the rising swirls of smoke and dust, we glanced round apprehensively, expecting the flash of a dagger or signs of a bomb. There were three of us—Bhaskar, Abbas and I. In our opinion, it was part of the traffic policeman's wicked design to keep us stranded there. Or, perhaps, there was a revolver digging into his back; which was why he couldn't move! Oof, the number of cars was unbelievable! They crawled forward in an unbroken line.

A few minutes later, the traffic policeman's taut arm relaxed to rest on his stomach and he stretched out the other. With a magic movement of his arm, the cars on our side of the road began to skid like restless fish. Jolted along over craters and bumps, in the midst of rumbling trucks and screeching gears, we were completing a thrilling escape, from the valley of cannibals, when the coal-tar road melted before our eyes and the wings of the birds gliding away began to get stuck in it.

Flutter, squirm, screech! Still pushing forward, trying to squeeze through, an even line drew up adjacent to us; unconcerned about how the cars already there would get through. Forming a third line, a heavy truck flew past, flapping its long wings, and went into a rut near the 'No Overtaking on the Bridge' sign. Shiny white grains of sugar bounced out on the ground like tiny diamonds. Other trucks in the line and a government jeep screeched to a halt. The women in the jeep were thrown forward, and, before they could regain their balance, the horse pulling the tonga behind the jeep pushed his repulsive nostrils into their lap! Screams of horror and repugnance! We got off our bikes and noticed that the youth from the jeep was lashing out with his belt at the horse and the tonga driver in turn—crack, crack! The tonga shook, like in an earthquake. Its driver screamed with pain, 'Sir, don't hit him! He's only a beast, sir! He can't apply brakes like you . . . .'

Crack!

'Oh! Oh! Do have mercy at least on the passengers!'

The peple in the tonga were clinging on for dear life. They were precariously perched; as if they would fall off any minute!

'Why must you drive the horse at such a speed if you can't control it?' Eyeing the women in the tonga, the sardar driving the truck scolded him.

'Run, you bastard, run!' A simultaneous outcry.

'Sir, as if there was room to run!'

His assailant turned round to have a look. In addition to a bus, hundreds of vehicles had lined up. Suddenly I remembered my friends. I started back to look for them. I found Abbas behind a few trucks, wedged between cars, holding on to his own bike and mine.

'I thought you'd gone too,' he said peevishly.

Leaving Abbas to look after the bikes, I moved forward again; this time to look for Bhaskar. The empty spaces in between vehicles were fast being filled by scooters and cycles. A new volcano was seething near the tonga. Boys had descended from the bus and were swearing at the jeep driver, threatening to kill him. Mindlessly, like sheep, the crowd was now on the tonga driver's side. Bhaskar was nowhere to be seen.

Skirting vehicles, I reached the overturned truck, but only human ants were visible there, falling on the scattered sugar. Bags, scarves, even pockets were being stuffed with sugar scraped up from the ground. The police! The police! No, it was not the police. These people dressed in khaki were from the fire brigade. They had swaggered into the throng of ants too. The truck had been carrying stolen sugar! The driver and his assistant were absconding. Searching for Bhaskar, my eyes returned after colliding with innumerable clusters of human ants, trucks and chassis of buses. I crawled forward. The tide of pedestrians was creeping forward, like me. On the lookout for Bhaskar, I was advancing haphazardly.

The traffic ahead was similarly jammed. There was an ambulance, in front. Chiefs of both armies, of the fire brigade and the ambulance, had pulled up next to each other. The ambulance driver grumbled, 'The bastards didn't even wonder how these cars would get through if they blocked the entire street! I've a delivery case on board, but as if they care!'

I propelled myself forward, pushing blindly, reading inscriptions on vehicles, hazarding a guess that this car was from Delhi, this one from Kanpur, this Calcutta, this one belonged to Sardarji, this to Singhji and this . . . it was futile, they were all the same.

'Didn't I tell you to pedal fast, faster . . . but did you listen? You went and got me stuck on the bridge, didn't you?' grumbled an obese Sethji, sitting alone in a rickshaw.

'Was it I who created this jam? You're just sitting back but I've lost two hour's earnings!' Having made his point, the rickshaw driver looked in front again.

'Water! Is there any water?' An appeal. Perhaps the man was sick. He got off the rickshaw and looked around.

'There's no water here. Yes, there's lots of water down there!' A taunt.

Startled, I examined my surroundings. That was the river below. Looking for Bhaskar, I had wandered very far.

'Here we are, suspended in mid-air! What better place could there be to drown?' A commentary.

I jerked around. No, it was not Bhaskar. It was a group of card players busy with a game.

'So many cars on the bridge! God forbid, what if the bridge were to collapse . . . ?' A comment with every card.

'Yes, that's what it says at the entrance—"The bridge is weak".'

'Did you know that last week, further down on this bridge, a truck broke through the railing and fell like a ball?'

'Really? Where was that?'

'There . . . just there.'

People peered down in alarm. Shadows dripped into the river.

'Nobody could have survived.' Nervousness.

'No, nobody did.' Fear rising out of jokes. Jokes born of fear.

'Don't talk like that. It's a bad omen . . . .'

The corpulent old *sethani* began to fumble hurriedly with the beads of her rosary. My eyes were tired of fumbling with the beads of human heads. It was with utmost difficulty that I could crawl forward. Had Bhaskar gone and done himself in?

'What a lovely spot!' A poetic being had discovered a piece of beauty even in this wretchedness. 'In the grey darkness, the expanse of the river has a colour all its own.'

This was enough incentive for a young girl in a station wagon to jump up and attempt to get a view. Tight jeans and a pink shirt were jarring to tired, dusty eyes.

'Papa, really a lovely spot; we're so lucky to be here!'

'I say, come inside! Come inside! Don't make a spectacle of yourself!' A middle-aged head screamed.

The spoilt one whined, 'Oh, no, Papa!'

A babble of taunts. The weather had become pleasant. The next instant the fairy was captive inside the station wagon. Fairyland was out of sight. The beautiful evening was melting into night. Somebody had switched on a transistor, perhaps to keep boredom at bay.

'Who can tell what might happen, surrounded by strangers as we are!' Apprehension.

'No, this melee would be enough to ward off miscreants.' Reassurance. One minute the crowd appeared hostile; then it changed into a friend, then a foe again, then . . . .

I had an impulse to head back but couldn't bring myself to abandon a friend in this wild city. It was a question of mutual security. I made a final attempt to scan the crowd. It reminded me of the rush on a railway platform. Rubbing against so many strange shoulders in the hope of finding a familiar one! I peered into each face, lost in the uncertain dusk. Out of the many heads floating in the flood, not one was familiar. I learnt that a peanut vendor had been hurt by a car door. His peanuts were being loaded on to the roof of the bus.

Plans were afoot to pass the peanut seller across, over the roofs of the cars, to the nearest hospital. The man from the truck stood on it and looked into the distance. It was packed on both sides! My feet landed on a sticky wetness. Was it petrol, diesel, the peanut vendor's blood or paan spat out by the owner of the car? By the time I could make up my mind, it seemed more important to turn back rather than move ahead.

'Oh, God, you've killed me!' Perhaps I had squashed somebody's foot with my shoe. So I was a torment for them too.

Begging pardon, I sidled forward past the trucks. One person's existence here was an impediment to another's.

'Watch out, bhai! Pickpockets are at large!' Fear crawled through my bones like lava. What if people took me for a pickpocket and fell on me? There was no reckoning with a crowd. I cursed Bhaskar, then myself, then Abbas.

'Waa! Waa!' Sethji jumped up in fright. He made an uncertain pronouncement regarding the cries of a newborn infant that were issuing from the ambulance. Raising himself on his toes, he was trying to peep inside.

'Did the crying infant give you a fright, Sethji! Who knows whether he'll turn out to be a timid cat or a tiger!' The rickshaw puller was amused. The ambulance driver was annoyed with the voyeurs.

'My dear people, have you no shame? What are you staring at?'

'Our own birth!' A stubborn reply. The ecstatic banging of mudguards, horns, bells! One sentence had made the man a hero! 'We've been stuck here for the last two hours. You never can tell what might happen!'

I moved forward in annoyance. A man was drinking water from a rubber tube attached to a truck. Was it that same man who was sick? I tried to figure out how far I was from the sugar truck. The geography had changed. A ghastlier situation than before—the stench of country liquor! There was a dishevelled drunkard on a rickshaw!

'Hey, you rickshaw fellow! Why are you shoving your rickshaw in here?' snapped an officer.

'Sir!' The rickshaw puller was taken aback.

'How much tax do you pay for the road?' A stern voice.

'What was that you said?' The drunkard came out of his stupor and stepped down from the rickshaw. Stumbling forward, he blazed out valiantly, 'Have you bought off the road? Or did your father bequeath it to you? You think you can pay more for the road today and push us out; tomorrow you'll pay more income tax and get our possessions auctioned, and next you'll get us thrown out of the country!'

A crowd had gathered. Many people had got off the bus. The officer was speechless with anger.

'How does a bastard get rich in this country? Ask me!' A second round of fire.

'Yes, come on, Manoj Kumar, tell us!' A performer emerged from the crowd.

'Look, don't swear at me or . . . if one is law-abiding and doesn't give some money as bribe, he can't get rich. A God-fearing, principled man can't get rich either. Of course, a patriot would kill himself rather than try to get rich in a land of beggars . . . .'

A consciousness of difference, of a sort of deprivation, had entered the rebel's speech. The officer had summoned a police constable and had set him on the drunkard. A kick on the bottom. 'Get lost, you bastard! Scram!'

'At least I pay for my drink, Mr Policeman; I'm not a freebooter like you!' Felled with the blow, the drunkard rose to his feet again. He took out a couple of rupees from his pocket and began to grovel.

'Come on, you bastard, I'll send you to jail.'

'Let me go just this once! If people like me didn't drink, how would you survive? Sterilization . . . prohibition . . . argh!' Vomit.

I couldn't bear the foul smell. Hell couldn't be worse!

Leaving the car stranded in the stench, the crowd had begun to disperse.

The policeman had shied off in the direction of the overturned truck. Taking advantage of his weighty presence, I followed in his footsteps. The effort cost me a graze on the elbow. I cursed myself, again.

The crowd of human ants was still gleaning grains of sugar. Banging the mudguards with his stick, the policeman grabbed somebody. 'Oy! Who's that killing himself on the mudguard?' A truck driver's sonorous tone.

Turning on his torch, the policeman pulled himself up to his full stature. 'These bastards have created this jam just to be able to loot. They behave as if they own this sugar and this street too.'

'What anarchy! Sugar is being stolen and the police stand and look on!' A taunt rose from the darkness like a bubble.

'Who's that? Come on out . . . not only do you steal, you're impudent to boot.'

'Pick up the bastard and throw him into the river!'

'Just because he's in uniform, he's throwing his weight around! Well, we're stuck here, in any case. Nobody's been able to get us out of this mess in the last three hours.'

The policeman looked sheepish and made a hurried attempt to lose himself in the throng, but there was no room to move and his effort seemed hilarious. He began to fumble in his pocket.

'What's wrong, Mr Policeman? How much was it?'

'Well, it certainly wasn't less than two hundred . . . .' The policeman's face was drained of colour.

'Do you collect that much in bribes in a day?'

'Imagine! A dacoit has been looted!'

The insecure keeper of security was compelled to endure the stings.

'Bhai, can you give me a bidi?' The policeman's arrogance had suddenly dissolved into an entreaty.

'Brother . . . . I can't believe it's the same person talking! You swore at me yesterday and are now calling me Bhai! If you'd been like this to begin with, why would this row have taken place?'

'Give it to me, *dost*!'

Swallowing his pride, the policeman was trying to become intimate with the rickshaw puller, like a bird flapping its wings and trying to break through a glass wall.

The jungle of vehicles had grown thicker. I was inching forward, holding on to the railing of the bridge. One slip and I would plunge into the river. Further ahead, some distance from the tide of people, I could discern seated shapes that, now, rose with the support of the railing. The mist cleared as I approached and I got a start . . . were these women sitting here in order to ease themselves? The sensation, so far asleep, of something sticky under my feet, awoke again. I rubbed my shoe against a tyre and wondered how to extricate myself from this mess. What was my place in this universe, and how was I to give meaning to my existence here?

Headlights shone as far as the eyes could see, creating glittering palaces of illusion. I thought of murky happenings in dark alleys, in houses and in humdrum localities. And what of bomb explosions that had become daily occurrences? There would be an uproar, police patrols and, then, the arrest of innocent people as a routine procedure. Terror glowed slowly in the lights of the illusory palace.

I did not notice when the lights melted away and I flowed forward in the tide of pedestrians. Rolling like a stone, I paused at a shore I recognized—wasn't that the same tonga driver? He wore a bandage now, but what was all that noise about . . . ? Who was that youth yelling at? Who was the fresh target of the whip?

'There are respectable women in the jeep. Tell me, sahib, is it good manners to switch on your lights and stare?' The tonga driver was now on the side of the youth.

'Who switched on his lights?'

'The sardar driver of that truck, who else?'

'Who tied your bandage?'

'Sahib did.'

'But isn't he the one who hit you?'

'Oh, he just did that because he was angry. Now my horse is an idiot, too. The ladies could have died of fright!'

Public opinion had become introspective by now. I changed my perspective accordingly, too.

The surging crowd acquired the momentum of a swing. People fell like houses, descending haphazardly on vehicles and other people. Taking advantage of the situation, the race to gain distance had commenced all over again. A riot had broken out. Aggressive trucks were moving ahead, crossing over the bodies of other vehicles.

The peace-loving protested ineffectively. The mood of the crowd was contagious—I found myself on top of the sardarji's truck.

'You're not going to listen, are you?' It was the sardarji's voice. A torch flashed sharply.

I descended; but people driving vehicles still eyed the pedestrians with suspicion. There had been some modification in the law of the jungle. The claws of the man-eaters and their sharp teeth were not a threat any more. No growls from them either. With drooping ears and tail, they were tolerating the excesses of the unruly pedestrians. But, then, the mob was stationary again and I was stuck in its midst. I called out to Abbas and then to Bhaskar, but heard other voices in reply.

The bridge was an island without law, discipline, direction or decision.

'After all, how did this jam come about? You're coming from that direction, aren't you?'

'A truck overturned in a rut.'

'Indeed, in this mad rush, it would have been surprising if it hadn't.'

'Every one is in a rush to get to their destination.'

'Sahib, I know where these truckers are going. If you go just a little further, there are brothels on both sides of the street. You'll find these trucks lined up there. That's why they're in a hurry to get away from here—pushing, crushing, not bothering about right or wrong—for, if there is a traffic jam near the brothel, then . . . .'

A flutter went through the crowd. 'Not quite, bhai, some trucks line up at the petrol pump, too. A procession was due to come out today, and the police intend to make some money at the check post, too . . . !'

'Hunh! A complicated situation, isn't it? The number of cars has gone up as well. You can't complain if they hit you, even if you don't possess a car yourself!'

'Bhai, you have to look for deeper reasons for the traffic jam! The price of sugar, oil, kerosene, the shortage of electricity, dearth of honesty . . . ! Deprivation! Action and reaction!'

'If you let problems multiply like weeds, there is bound to be a traffic jam one day.'

'Is there a bypass? A bypass . . . a . . . ?' The helpless fluttering of birds stuck in the coal tar! Tension was mounting. Eyes travelling to watches.

'Oof! Just for a little personal convenience, so many people have to tolerate this abominable situation!'

'Now, look, you're not supposed to overtake just where the signboard prohibits it. Naturally, the truck carrying stolen sugar overturned.'

'Didn't you read Vivekananda's teaching written on the truck— *"No big tasks are accomplished by means of cunning"*?'

'I could preach like that, too, if I occupied a position of power. Great people are often made into scapegoats to abet robbery.'

'Bhai, I can visualize what's going to happen to this civilization. Despite the fact that our civilization has attained a high level of culture, we'll be burnt to ashes like Bhasmasura because of our cunning; or maybe our vitality will change to shining, inanimate gold, as though touched by Midas.'

'That's true. Pushing and trampling blindly, where have we dragged civilization?'

'Stranded on this bridge, suspended in mid-air, what should we do now . . . ? All are destined to perish, whether guilty or innocent!'

An unwilling audience to this commentary, I rested my back against a taxi. A black curtain waved before my eyes. I was quite worn out. The fluttering of birds stuck on the coal tar was slowly dying out. Time froze like stone. Abbas was probably not far, holding on to my bike.

I closed my eyes and a world of relentless competition revolved in front of me, where men, vehicles, even houses, trampled each other, advancing menacingly like flood waters. The sensation of being buried alive within walls! We, the descendants of Bhasmasura and Midas, found it hard to avoid our own traps.

PAPER BULLETS
Abdul Bismillah

Dadi began to shout, even before day had broken, 'Najma, O, Najma! Fatima, O, Fatima! Will you get up now or are you going to hide under that quilt till it's ten o'clock? The call for prayer sounded long ago. Come on, up with you and be quick about it! Don't you want to work today? You'd better watch out! You'll get thrown out of your husband's place if you're lazy! Look at Bittan, what's she having to face. You've got no shame even when you've seen everything. O, Najma! Fatima!'

The girls emerged from under the quilt, giggling and calling their grandmother names. *Dadi* was in half a mind to wake up Wasiullah and make him give the girls a hiding, but, on second thoughts, she didn't. She ground a freshly folded paan in a pestle and put it in her mouth. Then, gently moving aside the dull green bandage that covered her right eye, she tried to take another look at the girls. She didn't approve of what she saw. Najma and Fatima were standing in the yard, laughing and pulling each other's hair. *Dadi* wished to say something again but couldn't bring herself to do so. She just sat there, back resting against the wall, silently cursing Wasiullah.

Wasiullah was her son. He lost his father when he was very little. However, she did not allow him to feel the loss, and, after educating him as well as she was able, she had set him up in a business of his own. But Wasiullah had no interest in work.

It was the election season and jeeps belonging to different parties could be seen moving around. The streets had come alive with different-coloured flags, and a variety of stickers shone on the candidates' shirts. Meetings were being held everywhere; new plans were made and happy days in the future were discussed again and again. Wasiullah loved all this. He was in the prime of his youth. He had married recently and the busy routine of work irked him. In the situation he found himself in, it was only natural ment doubled every time Haq Sahib visited the district, and he spent days and nights decorating the stage and making garlands. This kept him in the good books of Haq Sahib who considered him the only representative of the Muslim voters. Wasiullah could hardly contain his joy at the stature he had acquired.

He had fallen in the esteem of his wife, though. Perhaps it was this worry that had turned his hair prematurely grey and had pushed his health downhill. All he got to hear at home were taunts and, recently, he noticed that their standard of living had fallen. He suddenly realized that, for the past two years, he had had no means of income, and that his only son had left off studying to wander about aimlessly. All three of his daughters had reached puberty at more or less the same time.

Suddenly, now, two important duties loomed large in front of Wasiullah. He had to get his daughters married and set his son up in a job. Both tasks presented innumerable difficulties. Getting his son a job was, of course, nearly impossible, but he did manage to bluff his way through and find a husband for his eldest daughter. Though his son-in-law was also unemployed, Wasiullah reassured him that he was thick with Haq Sahib and would find him work after the wedding.

Soon, however, he began to get the feeling that Bittan's fate was doomed, though his wife disagreed with him on this point. According to her, if Bittan was unhappy, the reason was not her fate, but the promise Wasiullah had made which had not yet been fulfilled. She picked fights with Wasiullah Khan over this on a number of occasions.

Perhaps that was why he repeatedly raised the issue of reserving jobs for Muslims. After discussing the possibility of jobs for his son and son-in-law at every meeting with Haq Sahib, he immediately switched over to ruminating about the prospects of the entire Muslim community, and, Haq Sahib, chewing on a cashew nut, completely agreed with him. Holding a tray containing Haq Sahib's paan, Wasiullah Khan laughed obsequiously. His wife fretted at home. Najma and Fatima, oblivious of these happenings, discussed what clothes and sandals they would have for Id. Javed *Miyan* reclined in his room, absorbed in a detective novel. The family of a regional representative of the Muslims had fallen upon bad times.

Then, one day, there was a letter from Bittan: 'Respected *Abbajaan, Assalaam Alai Kum!* After I have said salaam, let it be known that, being well ourselves, we trust in God that you are in good health and are happy too. The reason for writing is that Babloo's papa has yet not been able to get a good job and the Rs 150 he gets from that private school is not enough to meet our needs. That is why he curses me all the time and threatens to divorce me if my father does not keep to his promise.'

The letter worried Wasiullah Khan. The girls stood like statues behind the torn curtain, and, Javed *Miyan*, abusing his father incoherently, went out. A strange desolation took hold of the house.

The next day Wasiullah Khan went to meet Haq Sahib, and his wife went into town. Somebody had told her that paper bullets for children's pistols were made there. You got a rupee for making a thousand bullets. If you worked very hard, it was possible to make four or five thousand bullets in one day. After all, Najma and Fatima needed something to do.

In this way, Najma and Fatima forfeited their freedom. They had earlier spent their time attending school, dropping in on friends, talking about their father and discussing fashions. Now they soaked paper at night, beat it to a pulp and settled down in the evening with the mould for making bullets. Their wrists got tired. Their arms felt like they'd drop off. But they knew that five or six people had to be fed off this. *Abbajaan* would not stop running after Haq Sahib. His wife had tried, on several occasions, to din it into him that he should give up his dependence on others and go about his own profession. Why not involve the son and the son-in-law in the family business? This set Wasiullah Khan's back up. 'Who asked you to lecture me? You think I'm going to set up shop now? What will people say? I've done so much for Haq Sahib. It's on my account that he got all the Muslim votes. Won't he do a little thing like this for me? He only has to pick up the phone. It's just that he's got a lot of things on his mind. Did you think he'd forget? He would have done this for me last time; unfortunately he was called away. Of course, he'll do it the next time. Even if he can't fix Javed up with a job, he'll definitely hunt one up for Lateef *Miyan*. Bittan didn't write again, did she?'

In fact, Wasiullah Khan's anger had waned while the conversation was in progress, and he had begun to think about Bittan. He knew she hadn't written. He looked at his wife's face intently and wondered whether he should ask Fatima to make some tea. However, his wife dashed cold water on any such ideas.

'She's written, but not to register any complaints. They are planning Babloo's circumcision. They've sent us an invitation.'

'Really?'

Wasiullah Khan cheered up momentarily, but his wife delivered another blow: 'You look happy at the prospect of going there, but have you thought of how you are going to face them? Will you go empty-handed again?'

Wasiullah abandoned the idea of tea and went out.

Things were slowly becoming clear to *Dadi* and she voiced a silent prayer, 'O holy God! Our honour is in your hands now. . . .' Though she knew that their honour was not in God's hands but in Najma's and Fatima's.

Khat! Khuta khat! Khat khuta khat! Najma and Fatima beat the paper relentlessly. Perhaps they were also beating their present, hoping to transform it into a better future. *Amma* had made it quite clear that they must arrange for their own dowry, and there was no better time to do it than the present. That was why they started collecting little things for themselves, too. Najma saved enough to buy a cheap watch and Fatima bought a few pots and pans. With the little they got from work, they embroidered pillow covers and handkerchiefs for their trousseau. Fans and tea cosies took shape under their fingers . . . . The girls were wearing themselves out in order to give some meaning to their own lives and to that of their family's. To add to it, they were also saving up for their elder sister's family.

'Did you laugh again?'

Najma and Fatima were giggling again. The pause in the '*khat khuta khat'* was evidence to this fact. *Dadi* disapproved of just this, and, adjusting the bandage on her freshly operated eye, she stood up. She couldn't climb the stairs, true, but she could at least go up to the stairs and shout at the girls. However, she saw that they were coming down. They were followed by their mother. It seemed they were going out. *Dadi* stopped short in her tracks. She muttered, 'This ogress ruined my son and now she's wrecking the girls! Dear God! Only you can help us!' She walked back to her place. She rummaged in her wicker basket for a paan but found only a stained rag there. There was no tobacco in her pouch either. She glowered and began to silently curse Wasiullah again.

There were two hand-carts outside. There was cheap jewellery and bric-a-brac on one and aluminium utensils were heaped up on the other. The girls were selecting earrings for themselves. *Amma* was examining a pot. The girls had no ornaments in their ears and *Amma*'s pot was worn out. She wanted to exchange this worn-out pot, a broken ladle and another damaged utensil for a new pan. The girls had taken a fancy to the earrings. Why, they looked as if they were made of gold!

'*Amma*, give us four rupees!' A smile played on Fatima's lips.

But *Amma* frowned. 'What for? We're not going to throw away money on those earrings! Go on, bhai! Don't get taken in by these girls. There's not a grain in the house and you expect me to produce . . . .'

The crestfallen girls returned the earrings and kept looking at the receding cart. They were sorry they had not put any money aside for themselves. They walked back slowly. *Amma* was showing off the new pan to *Dadi*.

It was the tenth of December. Babloo's circumcision was the day after. A bush-shirt and a pair of trousers had been bought for Lateef *Miyan*. Babloo's clothes had also been arranged for. Javed *Miyan* had been sent into town with the paper bullets. If he brought back some money, they could also buy a sari for Bittan. And, perhaps, shoes for the child, if there was still some money left over. Now, Lateef *Miyan* wouldn't sulk about a pair of shoes, would he? It would irk Bittan, no doubt; but it couldn't be helped.

'What are we going to wear, *Amma*? The clothes we got for Id are in tatters!'

Amma flared up at this. 'Why don't you ask your father who goes around thinking he's a minister? What can I say? I'm at my wits' end trying to meet the demands of the ceremony and you are worrying yourselves sick over fashions!'

Wasiullah stood outside, listening to his wife's outburst. He wished he could fly into a temper too, but found it difficult to rekindle the fire that had burned inside him before. Meeting Haq Sahib's demands had spent him. His face flushed and he walked out onto the street, towards the bus stop. Maybe he would catch Javed *Miyan* returning. However, Javed *Miyan* returned only at night. He brought the news that, with Deepavali being over, the price of bullets had fallen and the company had reduced the rates of labour. Things were really bad. It seemed they wouldn't even have the money now to meet food expenses.

Amma struck her forehead. *Dadi* hurled a string of abuses at the bullet company. Javed *Miyan* went off to take a nap. Wasiullah Khan stood rooted to the spot, and the girls searched the atmosphere, trying to gauge their own worth. Their arms felt like they'd drop off and they decided it was time to turn in for the night.

'Don't you want to make any more pulp?' Najma asked Fatima. Fatima refused. Her answer was monosyllabic and she curled up in bed. Najma was about to go and soak some paper, but then decided against it. She went to sleep too.

No one had expected Babloo's circumcision to go off successfully.... But an encouraging environment had been created with Wasiullah falling in with the ritual and being present there with his family. It seemed as if the bitterness between the son and Father-in-law was about to come to an end. However, a wave of unpleasantness went through the atmosphere when, at the last minute, Lateef *Miyan* refused to put on the clothes that had been brought for him.

'I shouldn't be forced to wear those clothes when I'm upset. I've no greed for clothing....What I do yearn for is the love I didn't get. I know that all was not well between us on account of that job, but you could still have kept in touch with me and enquired about how I was getting on! You stayed away from me because you were afraid I was annoyed. You couldn't care less about how I felt!'

Wasiullah's family stood around, like a group of mourners, listening to Lateef *Miyan*'s outpourings. Wasiullah was rearing to say something but couldn't get round to doing it. How could he explain that they had been far too ashamed to go there? Was it possible to convince Lateef *Miyan* that Haq Sahib had fooled him? And he could hardly admit that they found it difficult to make ends meet at their own place.

'Come on, son. Do try them on! Your wife's people have brought the clothes. It's bad manners to make such a fuss!' *Dadi* was trying to appease Lateef *Miyan* now, but he flared up even more.

'I don't accept my wife's people!'

Lateef *Miyan* jerked away *Dadi*'s hand and Javed *Miyan* took exception to this. 'Whom do you accept then?'

Javed *Miyan* spoke like the hero in a detective novel, and, Lateef *Miyan*, considering this unmannerly, lost his temper. 'Kindly watch what you say! It might be rented, but I'm certainly at my own place, not at yours, and if you don't know how to behave I'll have to ask you to leave. At once!'

He had finished everything with a single stroke.

The circumcision had been postponed; the crowd of guests had dispersed and Bittan's lips had trembled with unheard screams.

Wasiullah stood outside, waiting for a rickshaw with his family. His mother, his wife, Najma, Fatima, Javed . . .with their broken attaché cases and grimy bags; they appeared to be futile and weak. As though they were not people but big bullets of paper littered on the street . . . soggy, of no use and entirely defenceless!

THE GOLDEN WAIST-CHAIN
Uday Prakash

Darkness would descend on the house at night. Somehow it was much deeper than in other houses. The walls were quite submerged in it. The air became thick and crowded with a hundred smells. Often it seemed to me to carry the fragrance of the *kewra* flower, even though there was no *kewra* tree in the entire village. Sometimes it had an odour of the fish that teemed in the lake outside our village. Fish sweat pushed its way into our lungs, our breathing became heavy and we sensed a strange dampness in the air.

At times, a fetid smell settled like a thin layer over the whole house, and, with it, the shadow of an unseen fear. *Amma* would say, 'Looks like there's a dead rat somewhere.' Her voice became tinged with indecision and fear. Then, as though reassuring herself, she softly said to me, '*Munna*, go to the dark room and see what *Dadi* is up to.'

It would at once become clear to me that *Amma* was again gripped by the fear she associated with that smell, and was struggling with misgivings about *Dadi*. All of us often forgot about *Dadi* and sometimes it was months before we set eyes on her. Because she was not physically present before us, she had no substance in our memory.

We called the room, in which *Dadi* lay sleeping, on her old sheesham cot, the 'dark room'. It was a very small narrow hole sunk into the ground and had no windows. It had just a tiny door with a beam so low that one had to almost sit down to descend into the room. The floor of the room was at least a foot and a half below ground level. It was always dark inside, even in the day. *Dadi* didn't emerge from it for days, and, sometimes, even for months. Perhaps she urinated in some corner of that room too, for the acrid stench of ammonia was always present in the thick, closed air of that dark hole. *Dadi*'s whole being gave off a similar smell.

It was my belief that *Dadi* could see perfectly well in the darkness of the room. At times, when *Amma*, frightened by the rotting smell, asked me to peep in on *Dadi*, I saw two light grey eyes burning in the gloom which held *Dadi*'s cot. A cat's eyes glow in the same way. When I called out, '*Dadi*, O *Dadi*!' a rasping voice would issue from those eyes. I ran back in the dark and yelled, '*Amma*, *Dadi* is still alive!' At this *Amma* gave me a dressing-down. If I said, '*Amma*, *Dadi* isn't rotting; something else must have died,' *Amma* scolded me again. This was why, whenever the familiar smell spread through the house, and *Amma* sent me to look in on *Dadi*, I sang out, '*Dadi* says, "I'm here!" '

At night I was afraid of cats, though—especially of the black cat that came only at night, climbed down from the roof, roamed the entire house and sometimes sat down under my bed. This cat had grey, burning eyes too. They gave off a dirty yellow light. The darker the night, the clearer would those shining eyes be. When the cat wailed at night, I was confirmed in my conviction that she was none other than *Dadi*. Maybe she adopted this disguise so that she could get a feel of our house. The women in our village often told tales of ladies who knew the art of casting spells and could transform themselves into any object. They practised black magic and their favourite form was the cat, because cats can see in the dark.

In those days it wasn't just *Dadi*, every woman was an object of wonder for me. I was constantly suspicious, always on the lookout for a woman in the act of metamorphosis. I was unsuccessful, though. I could not even chance upon *Dadi* becoming a cat.

Chachi, it was popularly believed, had a square block of wood in place of her heart. She had this installed when *Chacha* ran away from home and she didn't even have a child to console her. She was very cruel. *Chachi* had once told me that, long ago, when *Dadi* was young and very beautiful, she had become friends with a barber's wife. This woman knew how to cast spells and *Dadi* had taken some lessons from her. However, a spell can sometimes rebound on the one who casts it. This is precisely what happened to *Dadi*. Her body, once so tender as to blister the minute she stepped out into the sun, and which gave off the scent of *bela* flowers on summer nights, had first turned copper-coloured and, then, brown; all on account of that spell going back on her. She had given birth to thirteen children, of whom only Pitaji, my *bua* from

Jasidih and *Chacha* had survived. According to *Chachi*, it was *Dadi*'s imperfect spell that gobbled up all her children. It was also the influence of *Dadi*'s black magic that Pitaji and *Chacha* could never stay put at home.

Ours was a feeble, sick and slowly disintegrating house. Every plank of the roof, each beam and edge, had been besieged by woodworms that were busy all day, dropping white sawdust down below. Every object and corner of the house was buried under that fine powder. When *Amma* swept the house in the evening, one corner of the yard was piled high with sawdust, dirt and rubble.

Amma knew that the walls of the house had become hollow and in it existed a different world, with its own kind of life. Rats inhabited this world, as did strange insects of motley hues and other invisible creatures we never got to see. Perhaps this world had its own set of rules and it got its sustenance, air and fuel from our outside world. We all knew that our house was advancing slowly towards ruin. It could, at any moment, meet with a sudden death. In the silence of the night, when the stale smell of fish would envelop the house, strange, high-pitched sounds could be discerned from inside the walls. It created the illusion of somebody softly whispering, in an unfamiliar and incomprehensible tongue. These voices talked about fate and death in our world. The sounds of many things being broken and rebuilt could be heard. Something new was being forged and created there. Sometimes it seemed as though, in the vast hollow of the walls, a gigantic python lay asleep, and its hot, vaporous breath swept across our lives and dreams.

The cat, *Dadi* and black magic were not the only things I was afraid of. I was frightened of the walls too. I was convinced that if I stood with my ear to the wall, the mysteries of that other world would be revealed to me. However, my heart began to hammer loudly and I could not summon the courage to listen to the unseen, obscure language of that other world. I felt that, if by a stroke of chance I understood the meaning of even a single word, I would definitely not remain alive.

It was my surmise, however, that *Dadi* not only understood that tongue, many events in that world took place at her command. The invisible threads of misfortune and tragedy that led our house to destruction were tied to her fingers. What, after all, was she up to for months on end, in that dark hole? *Dadi* was our enemy. She knew this too; and we, of course, knew it well. She knew, too, that, but for Rame, my father, no one could make head or tail of what she said. She had lived for eighty years and was now engrossed in a magical game that would finish us off along with her. It was the effect of that magic that our house was eighty years old, too, and we all felt our lungs and bones to be eighty years old. We wanted to save ourselves from extinction.

Dadi had only one meal a day. Rice, dal, chutney and dried chillies were placed in a battered old metal pot and *Amma* left this on the threshold of the dark room. Often, for a whole week, the pot returned untouched, and then nobody would eat that food. We would forget completely about *Dadi*. No one so much as mentioned her. It went on like this for months. Then, one day, in the corner of the yard where *Amma* piled up the rubbish, *Dadi* was noticed sitting on that mound in her dirty white sari, her forehead resting on her palms. *Chachi* immediately commented on this: 'The old crone has emerged again today; you can take it from me someone will be taken ill.'

A peculiar sense of quickness and activity took hold of the house as soon as. *Dadi* emerged. *Chachi* grumbled incessantly. *Bua* stamped past *Dadi*. *Amma* swept the house in a frenzy, throwing old rags, broken bits and pieces out into the yard. Everyone pretended not to see *Dadi*. I knew it well, though, that it was *Dadi*'s presence outside today that put the house in such turmoil, as though it were a basin that held turbulent water. It was on account of her that everyone was acting so busy. They spoke to each other in loud voices. I was sure that this was not the usual bustle of activity but only a changed expression of the animosity that everyone nursed against *Dadi*. The minute she showed up outside, the whole house began to sway like a boat and rose up against her like an army.

Dadi used to remain sitting on the gunny bag that she had spread out on the heap of rubbish. At times she could be seen stitching a bag. Once, I remember, she caught my eyes on her face and her wrinkles dissolved into an extremely helpless smile. She motioned me to come to her. This was, perhaps, her first and only reaction to the external world. Maybe she wanted me to thread the needle for her. However, I stayed away. I was afraid she might surreptitiously stick that black magic hair of hers on me. *Chachi* had once warned me that these voodoo women sometimes stick a hair from their head on to children. Later they use trickery to call that hair back; whereupon they dip it in a bowl of milk. The milk immediately turns into blood. This blood belongs to no one else but that child. I had good reason to be scared. In case this happened to me, my body would turn white like a sheet of paper.

Dadi looked like an old vulture who had lost all its hair and had only a gaunt, sickly, wrinkled neck and a bald head. The brain inside this skull listens softly to the murmuring of its last days. I sometimes felt sorry for *Dadi*, but she was our foe. She had a waist-chain of gold that weighed five-hundred-and-sixty grams and she had buried this away, somewhere, maybe in the house, under the floor or inside the walls, perhaps near the well at the back of the house or under a nearby tree.

At night, the day's work being done, *Chachi*, *Bua* and *Amma* gathered round the lantern. It was the only one in the house. *Amma* ate her meals only when she was finished with washing the dishes, after everybody else had eaten. She carried her food over to the lantern, scrutinized closely each bit of chapati she broke off, picked out and threw something from it and, then, chewed on it for ages. She continued to talk all the while. After she got married, *Bua* had gone away to Jasidih, which is near Orissa, but within a year of her wedding she lost her husband and was back at our place. That was ten years ago. She had remained with us ever since. She said everything in a tone of surprise, which is why her eyes were always wide open. Looking at her one got the impression that the world was an amazing place for her indeed, and all that it held was enigmatic.

Chachi was small in stature and very skinny. She was childless, though her age could not have been less than fifty. Since she had a piece of wood where her heart should have been, she was very cruel. One day she had branded my arm with a red-hot iron and provoked *Amma* into a fight. I think that was the day when *Amma* told me about the block of wood.

Considering how dark our house was, the murky light of the lantern obviously did not suffice. Night drowned the objects in the house in viscous air, in obscure odours and mysterious sounds. The world inside the hollow walls would spring into life, and a sense of those unseen movements would come through to us as we sat huddled around the lantern. The conversation between *Amma*,

Bua and *Chachi* appeared to be interminable and presented itself to my mind as the interchange from an immense story. Listening to them, I made a silent decision to write the story of that house when I grew up.

With her mouth full of food, *Amma*'s face seemed aged and frail by the uncertain light of the lantern. She said, 'If only *Dadi* would part with the waist-chain, this house could yet be saved.'

Chachi's reply to this was, 'You can take it from me, when the old hag dies, the waist-chain will come out of her intestines. She'll never let us in on the secret so long as she lives.'

Amma's face darkened, 'May God deliver us from such avarice which blinds us to the love of our fellow human beings.'

Bua quite often said nothing. It occurred to me, with surprise, that *Dadi* was *Bua*'s *Amma*. Apparently *Dadi* had forgotten everyone; *Bua*, Rame and *Chacha* too. The whole world was an unfamiliar place to her. Perhaps all she was acquainted with now was the mystic language of the world within the walls. Since she did not remember our language, no one understood what she said.

Pitaji was the only one who sat and talked to her for hours in the dark room, on the very first day of his return from Calcutta. *Dadi* was his mother. She was the one who had given him birth.

The waist-chain that weighed five-hundred-and-sixty grams had been bought by *Dada*. *Dada*, too, was an actor in the story of our house. He was widely travelled and had accomplished much. The way I saw it, all the world knew about him. His picture, long faded, hung in *Amma*'s room. That was the only picture we had, clinging to a bit of glass and slowly disintegrating with the effect of time and weather. *Dada* wore a Maharashtrian turban on his head, balanced a gun on his thigh and had enormous moustaches.

By the light of the lantern, any mention of the golden waist-chain started off the story of *Dada*, too. According to *Amma*, *Dada*'s favourite hobby was keeping birds as pets. He was friends with each duck in the village and had endowed the birds with individual names. He even brought them home sometimes. Then the house would be milling with ducks! Quite a catastrophe! *Dada* knew precisely which bird had fledglings on a particular branch of a certain tree in the forest, and how old the fledglings were now. His friendships were not confined to ducks alone; he conversed with crows and bullocks too. Often he could predict, quite correctly, by looking at ants, whether it would rain or not.

As it happened, an English officer was in the habit of coming with his white woman and his twelve-bore gun to shoot birds at that very lake where *Dada*'s cranes, ducks, guinea-fowl, sandpipers, moorhens and God knows what else lived. *Dada* returned sadly on occasions and declared, 'Today the white man killed Mohan, Sawant and Dooji.'

Amma relates how he lay on his cot one evening, watching Jupiter, Venus and Saturn just appearing, when the orange-blue sky had suddenly begun to swarm with birds. All the birds in the world, maddened, were screaming in the sky. A guinea-fowl fell near *Dada*'s feet. She was bathed in blood, her body riddled with bullets and her neck slit in half. *Dada* cleaned and loaded his gun, fixed his turban on his head and set off towards the lake.

Dada, it is said, stood on the embankment of the lake, facing the English officer, and told him that it was an offence to shoot game at that lake. He said that all the birds at that lake were his domestic pets and that he did not want the Englishman coming there to shoot again. Because the Englishman had come only with his wife that day, he left without a word. The next day, however, *Dada*'s fields were confiscated, his animals herded away and our village was declared traitorous.

Now the English officer turned up every evening and shot birds with his twelve-bore. *Dada* would lie on his cot in the yard and watch the sky fill with birds; bloodied guinea-fowl, wounded ducks, screaming lapwings and frightened storks. According to *Amma*, the day the furious English officer fired at the ducks in the lake was the same day when shots were fired in Jallianwalla Bagh in Punjab.

Once more *Dada* cleaned his gun and sat hidden behind mango leaves on the other embankment of the lake. The English officer was there with his wife and his henchmen. He sat in his canopy built on a mango tree.

Dada's voice rung out, 'That is the last time you shoot here, you son of a lord! I am the master of the lake and of the birds and this is my command. . . .'

Because *Dada* sat obscured by the leaves of the mango tree, he was hidden from the Englishman's view. Perhaps they thought it was their own fear that led them to imagine that voice. The officer was outraged. The English were the sovereigns of India at that time, and here was *Dada* daring to question their right to duck-shooting!

The officer aimed at a flock of guinea-fowl from his canopy. . . . Bang! The gun went off and the sky darkened with shrieking birds. However, it was not dead guinea-fowl that rained down this time; what fell was the body of the English officer.

Two triggers had gone off simultaneously. *Dada* descended from the embankment, and, after he had cleaned the nozzle of his gun, he cast a glance at the birds and smiled. Then, waving his hand in farewell, he ran away. After which there was no sign of him for twenty-five years; so *Amma* relates. Rumour had it that he had become a hermit. In other stories about him, he was a dacoit. His fields had been confiscated already. There was nothing to eat in the house. *Dadi* was single-handedly raising three children—that is, Pitaji, *Chacha* and *Bua*. According to local gossip, *Dada* had fled to Germany and thence to Russia; he had swum out to sea and punctured the bottom of an English liner; he had looted a train. Others felt he had been killed in an encounter; perhaps he had been hanged. It was possible, too, that he had contracted cancer and died.

However, he returned home on a Thursday evening in November, just a day before Deepavali, twenty-five years later. He was now old and frail. A white beard covered his face and he was bald. It is said that on the night of the Deepavali festival, he gave *Dadi* the waist-chain that weighed five-hundred-and-sixty grams. It was of solid gold.

The year *Dada* returned coincided with the one in which India gained independence. However, he fell ill the same year. It was said of him that, when he had been strong and well, he had once stopped a moving railway engine and had pushed it back for one-and-a-half miles along the tracks. In the days after independence, though, he did not have the energy to lift up even the pot that he carried with him to the toilet. Because he suffered from asthma, he was constantly short of breath. Pitaji, *Chacha* and *Bua* were grown-up by this time. *Bua* was of the opinion that, the year India gained independence, all those who had fought against the British gradually fell ill and died. *Dada* died that year too. In his last days, hordes of flies swarmed over his face which was sticky like a ball of jaggery.

Dada looked like an aged vulture, too, but he had forgotten the language of the birds. He had visited the lake the day he came back but not one duck recognized him. What happened was that all the older ducks had died and, to the new generation, *Dada* was a total stranger. Something had broken inside him when he realized this fact. 'Everything has changed. . . ,' was all he said. The brass pot, in which he had carried water to the toilet, was still in our storeroom. It was too heavy for me to lift.

The faces of *Amma*, *Chachi* and *Bua*, by the ailing yellow light of the lantern, resembled the pale pictures in some ancient motheaten book.Their voices floated for a while on the air which was dense with the perspiration of fish and, then, passed into a wet nothingness. We were all aware of the fact that our house was now slowly changing to dust. *Amma* was becoming dust, too. Pitaji managed to come home only a couple of times in the year. He worked as a clerk in a cloth shop belonging to a Marwari merchant in Calcutta. *Chacha*, earlier, had visited us more frequently, but this time he had not shown up for the last four years. Sometimes he sent a money order worth fifty rupees.

He had kept an Assamese woman, who ran a green-grocery, as his mistress in Gauhati. I heard *Amma* and *Bua* talking about it. She was supposed to be very beautiful and knew black magic. *Chacha* had just to think about returning home and she turned him into a bull and tied him to a post. *Bua* felt that, if only *Chachi* had given birth to a child, *Chacha* would definitely have come home. Look at Pitaji, didn't he come back? Once Pitaji said something about taking me to Calcutta with him, but he dropped the idea because he didn't have a room there. He'd been sleeping in the merchant's shop for the past twelve years.

One day Pitaji had also asked *Dadi* about the waist-chain that weighed five-hundred-and-sixty grams. *Dadi* didn't speak for a very long time. Then she said, 'Rame, when your *Baba* killed the foreigner and ran away, I had a hundred grams of gold. I alone know what hard times I had to face in order to bring up my three children and educate both of you boys. I had forty grams of gold left over which I divided between my two daughters-in-law. How you've paid me back, son, can be seen not only by God, but the whole village as well.' *Dadi* had begun to weep at this and had then continued, 'My daughter-in-law at least keeps rice and dal for me at the door. What expectations will they have left of me if I give away the waist-chain? Whether the waist-chain exists or not, it is essential for both of us because it keeps your interest alive in me, son.'

Chacha and Pitaji had ransacked the entire house. They had consulted an astrologer and dug the ground in various spots; they had even used occult knowledge in order to find the hidden treasure, but the place where *Dadi* had concealed the waist-chain was anybody's guess. Once *Amma* dreamt that a bronze pot, containing the waist-chain, had been buried under the little platform of the tulsi tree in our yard, and that three white serpents were guarding it. The platform had been taken apart.

Once, on the day of the Teej festival, *Dadi* was dumped in the yard, bed and all. *Bua* massaged her with mustard oil. Her hair was combed out and made into a bun. *Amma* cooked potatoes and cauliflower, especially for her, and fed her puris, halwa and kheer. She was fanned so that she may stay cool. *Bua*, *Chachi* and *Amma* tried to extort the information from her in all kinds of subtle and devious ways. All this time, Pitaji was digging in the dark room with a pick-axe, but the waist-chain was nowhere to be found.

Once, *Dadi* got a heatstroke. She didn't surface from the dark room for several days. She only groaned.

Of course, *Chachi* had that block of wood where her heart should have been. She said, 'Now is the time! If the old witch tells us the whereabouts of the waist-chain now, it'll be fine. You never know when she may breathe her last!'

Chachi, it is said, intimidated *Dadi* even during her illness. She flashed a knife at her, throttled her and tried to suffocate her by gagging her. Unable to breathe, *Dadi*'s body blew up like a balloon, but, even under such pressure, she refused to reveal the whereabouts of the waist-chain.

Then she was starved for a whole month. *Amma*, *Chachi* and *Bua* discussed, within her hearing, how every brick of the house was being sold, and no one had a morsel to eat as Rame had stopped sending money. Gold doesn't travel to heaven with anyone. Yama, the God of Death, snatches it on the way and shoves it into the stomach of a buffalo. Or else, it simply remains behind on earth. And gold, which is hoarded away while a child starves, turns into excrement. It is eaten up by termites.

I don't know if *Dadi* heard all this. She was our adversary. Pitaji sometimes burst out in anger, 'It is all of you who see *Amma* as an enemy. I dread to think of what you'll do to me when I'm decrepit and old. Well, I can tell you, right away, that I have no wealth stacked away. I burn my blood to look after all of you. Please have mercy on me . . .!' One day Pitaji said, 'There is no waist-chain. It is all make-believe. Baba went neither to Rangoon nor to Germany. It has come to light that he worked in a brick kiln in Calcutta. My mother was born eating tobacco. Being such an addict, if she had the waist-chain, she would have sold it long ago to buy tobacco! It is all a pack of lies. There is no waist-chain anywhere.'

Amma wept late into that night. Then she wept incessantly for days on end, while she cooked and washed the dishes and swept the place. She was scared. It was only the miracle of the waist-chain weighing five-hundred-and-sixty grams that could have saved our house from disintegrating to sand; from being extinguished. Father's body was giving way too. Had there been no waist-chain, the dust collected over the years, the woodworms and the magical world inside the walls would long have transformed our house into a hill of mud wherein our bones would have been buried, and our future too.

The time Pitaji said the waist-chain was non-existent, *Amma* had wept for twenty-five days and, for the same number of days, *Chachi* had thrown grit in *Dadi*'s food. Pitaji had returned to Calcutta the same night and a darkness, thicker and blacker than coal, had descended over the house. The lantern would splutter and go out. A rank stench, as of something dying, was everywhere. On one occasion, when *Amma* sent me to peep into the dark room, I saw *Dadi*'s light eyes glowing in the dark. She was moaning. It stank of urine in there. The battered metal bowl containing the gritty rice and dal stood on the threshold. A terrible battle was being waged in our house. *Dadi* was on one side and everybody else on the other. I wasn't quite sure which side I was on.

The black cat walked the house at night. Through the day, the woodworms dropped sawdust from the thatch till all was shrouded under that fine powder. When we woke, we found our sheets, our hair and eyebrows covered. *Amma*, *Bua* and *Chachi* swept the house many times a day. A high stack of wood, dirt and rubble was always piled up in a corner of the yard. Then, one day, *Dada*'s picture fell by itself from the wall, and, we noticed with amazement and horror, that *Dada*'s face was no more in the frame. Instead there were insects of varying sizes with shining golden backs. They had eaten away the wooden frame too. I saw that *Dada*'s brass pot was missing from the store-room.

The women of the village talked amongst themselves and said that the old woman had been placed in pure hell by her sons, daughter and daughters-in-law. May God call one away before one meets with such a fate.

There was another picture of *Dadi* in my memory. The war in our house was not so fierce then and *Dadi* was not as old either. She had produced a wooden elephant on wheels and a ball from her bag and had given them to me. *Dadi* used to sing a holy song, too, which was difficult to explain: '*Hai dit Rama . . . hai dit Rama.*' This memory went back many years. It did not connect with the *Dadi* of today. Now *Dadi* had forgotten she even knew me. Maybe she took me for an enemy, too, and had discarded me from her memory. She had forgotten every one. The language of this world as well.

Dadi was never fond of rice. She came from the North. Whenever she cooked rice for *Dada*, she made chapatis for herself, too. Yet, her metal pot always contained rice. Her supplies of tobacco were long finished. Nothing that she liked was left in the world any more. If it was, it was inaccessible to her. All is fair in war. Every weapon was tried on *Dadi*. *Dadi* was equally untiring in her job of finishing off our house by way of curses and sorcery. Sometimes it seemed as though *Dadi* was losing, and would have to fling the waist-chain weighing five-hundred-and-sixty grams out into the yard, and the combat would be resolved at last. Then it appeared that *Dadi* would win anyway. It was on account of her that our house was decrepit and shaky to its foundations. Her legions, consisting of darkness, cat, wind, woodworms, mice, disease and ill-tidings, were conducting the conflict with great determination. *Bua*'s husband was dead; *Chacha* had been made into a bull by the Assamese woman; Pitaji couldn't get away from work for months; *Chachi* was barren; it did not rain. All our four fields had been sold. The last bit of land at the back of the house had been mortgaged. *Dada*'s brass pot had been sold, too, and his photograph had been swallowed by shiny bugs. *Dadi* was definitely winning.

That evening *Dadi* appeared from the dark room. *Chachi* had deprived her of food for ten days. *Dadi* resembled a sick skeleton that somehow managed to stay on its feet. Her body emitted a stench of urine. She squatted on the pile of debris without even spreading out her gunny bag. Her hairless head was bare. Below it, a long, emaciated, wrinkled neck. Her eyes were sunk into two cavities and seemed to gaze not outwards but in.

The head that grew on the skinny neck quivered and water flowed from the two holes that held the eyes. Her entire frame shook. Her hands fluttered like leaves in the wind. I saw that the sight of her frightened *Bua*, who said to *Amma*, 'I think *Dadi* has a touch of malaria. She is trembling with the fever.' *Amma* looked at *Dadi* through the open window of the kitchen.

There she sat in a corner of the yard, on top of all that piled-up rubbish, like an ailing, ancient vulture. She sang deliriously, '*Hai dit Rama . . . hai dit Rama . . . .*'

Chachi said, 'The old woman looks like she'll die. This is our last chance. We must have our wits about us or we're finished! If she doesn't give it to us now, the house will be a wreck!'

I saw *Chachi* go up to *Dadi*, take hold of her arm and hoist her up. *Dadi*'s arm was a bag of bones under an ancient, shiny, scaly skin. She sang continuously, '*Hai dit Rama. . . hai dit Rama. . .* a pot without a base doth roll . . . a pot without a base doth roll. . . *hai dit Rama . . . .*'

Chachi had her mouth close to *Dadi*'s ear and she was shouting, 'O, *Dadi*, Rame has wired to say that he is very sick. He has a tumour, weighing one-and-a-half kilos, in his stomach. He has no money for an operation. *Dadi*, tell us where the waist-chain is, or he will die.'

Meanwhile, *Amma* had come up. She held on to *Dadi*, too. She yelled in *Dadi*'s ear: '*Dadi*, Rame will not survive. *Munna* is dying too. Let us have the waist- chain.'

It was clear, however, that *Dadi* had completely forgotten the language of this world. Her naked head trembled, water flowed from the depressions that held her eyes, her hands shook like dry leaves, and an incessant refrain issued from her toothless mouth: '*Hai dit Rama. . . hai dit Rama. . . .*' She had lost her senses and drifted into a coma.

Then *Chachi* screamed, '*Behan*, just look down! It looks like *Dadi* has got diarrhoea!'

It was true. *Dadi*'s dirty sari was soiled and yellow excreta was spreading in the yard. A strong stench of urine emanated from her body. A putrid smell pervaded the whole house. I felt nauseous. *Dadi*'s sullied form shook with fever, '*Hai dit Rama. . . hai dit Rama. . . .*'

Bua brought a bucket full of water, which *Chachi* poured over *Dadi*. *Dadi*'s filthy sari clung to her skeleton. There was a slimy foul mess in the yard. The stench gained in intensity.

Chachi was still shouting in *Dadi*'s ear, '*Dadi*, can you hear me? Rame is dying. So is *Munna*. Produce it now at least! Give it to us! O *Dadi*!'

A second, third, and then a fourth bucket of water splashed over *Dadi*. The tremors seemed to go away. Her neck had slumped forward. She had stopped singing. *Amma* and *Chachi* carried her back to the dark room. But the room smelt so foul that they found it impossible to remain there.

Chachi said, 'The old woman can change her own clothes. Didn't you notice, sister, how much vigour she still has in those old bones? Two people couldn't manage to prop her up! The old witch must have drunk the elixir of eternal life! She won't go so easily.'

For the first time I saw *Bua*'s face sad and tense: 'I think it's different this time. *Dadi* never behaved like this.'

That night the black cat was nowhere to be seen. The lantern was shedding more light than usual. There was neither the rotting smell, as of something dying, nor the heaviness of fish sweat in the air. In fact, a couple of times, I had the illusion that I smelt *bela* flowers. It was a beautiful night, as light as paper. I had a good sleep that night. The world inside the walls also slept, for a change. *Bua*, *Chachi* and *Amma* were still deep in conversation when I drifted off to sleep.

In the morning *Chachi* came running out into the yard. Her face was white as a sheet. She stood in the middle of the yard and called out to *Amma*, '*Behan*, come here at once! *Dadi* is no more. I've just been to the dark room!'

Amma left the dishes, and, having thrown some water into the stove to put it out, she came out into the yard. Then the sound of *Bua* weeping began to rise up into the air. Like music. Soon the village women started pouring in. The yard was full. The house resounded with lamenting voices. I was crying, too, and at the same time quietly trying to catch one of these women in the act of changing herself into something else. I could not find the courage to go towards the dark room, even though I was curious to have a peek inside. You never know, maybe *Dadi*'s light eyes would still be glowing in the dark and her rasping voice would growl out a reply when I called out. . . I also had a desire to have a look at the metal bowl in which *Dadi* ate her meals and in which *Chachi* used to throw dust and grit.

Dadi had been cremated by the edge of the pond by the afternoon. The air had a distinct smell of *kewra*. The python inside the walls was blowing out steam no more. However, a few times I did imagine I heard the thin, piping sound of *Dadi*'s song from in there: 'Hai dit Rama. . . hai dit Rama . . . .'

Pitaji arrived on the seventh day. A wire had been sent to *Chacha*, too, but he neither came nor sent a reply. The Assamese woman had definitely turned him into a bull.

It was on the evening of the tenth day after *Dadi*'s death that Pitaji entered the dark room. It was impossible to recognize the objects that were found in *Dadi*'s little bundle now. Apart from four or five dried black guavas, there was also a black wooden ball, which, many years ago, must have been of rubber. One bag contained a little horse on wheels, which was once wood, but now coal. Another little bundle held two balls of jaggery which had crumbled to dust. The rest were tattered clothes. This was all that *Dadi* possessed.

Chachi had thoroughly swept out the dark room. *Dadi*'s cot had been thrown into the lake, from where the *doma* must have retrieved it. Pitaji was digging away at the floor and the walls of the dark room with a pickaxe. *Amma* was counting the beads of her rosary to facilitate the finding of the waist-chain. *Bua* was using a basin to throw out dug-up earth from the dark room. There was an unceasing noise of Pitaji going at it with the pickaxe. The smell of burning incense and *ajwain* pervaded the house.

Chachi cradled me in her lap. 'Now all will be well. The scourge of the house is no more. You wait and see, we will soon find the waist-chain.'

This meant that *Dadi*'s magic was about to fade. *Dadi* was dead and we would win now. Our house would not dissolve into dust. The thatch would be changed. The hollow walls would be filled up with cement and mortar. We would get our four fields back. Pitaji would give up being a clerk at the merchant's shop and live with us; the land at the back of the house would be returned to us; *Chacha* would return from Gauhati; the Assamese woman would do the dishes at our place and work in the fields; I would start school; *Amma*'s illness would be treated; the air would be fragrant with *kewra,* and there would be many lanterns in the house, even a torch. . . .

Amma was reading aloud from the holy book. *Bua* was still throwing out dug-up earth. A little hillock of mud had grown up there. It was getting to be night. *Chachi* sat near me. I did not know when I fell asleep.

I was woken in the middle of the night by loud wails. *Amma* and *Bua* were weeping noisily. Mounds of stones, bricks and dug-up soil became visible in the murky light of the lantern. Pitaji's mobile form could be seen on the other side. He held the pickaxe in his hand. He was through with digging the walls and floor of the dark room and was now advancing, digging in the direction of the house. Like a destructive demon. Thud! Thud! Went the pickaxe. I was frightened. I had never seen Pitaji like this. He was covered with grime. A shout escaped his throat each time the pickaxe fell.

I had begun to weep out of sheer fright.

Chachi spoke softly, 'I wonder what has possessed *Jethji*? It must be the effect of the black magic that the old crone practised in the dark room. It's only since he came out of there that his eyes have been red and he's behaving strangely. . . . O God, save us now!'

Pitaji moved forward as he dug. The lantern spluttered. We could smell something dead in the air. The mysterious sounds inside the walls had come alive again. Quick sounds of activity could be discerned. Things were being forged and others broken in there. I noticed that the woodworms had dropped so much sawdust that my sheet, hair and eyebrows were shrouded. *Chachi, Amma* and *Bua* were all submerged under it. The floor of the house, too, was collecting the fine powder. The lantern had spluttered and gone out. In the blackness which held the dark room, and, from where Pitaji was now advancing, digging, two light eyes could be seen burning steadily.

A little later, the black cat started roaming the house. Occasionally, its whimpers would unite with those of *Bua's* and *Amma's*

GLOSSARY

Aapa	respectful form of address for elder sister in Muslim families
Abbajaan	father in Muslim families
Abhimanyu	one of the heroes of the epic *Mahabharata*
ajwain	an aromatic seed
Babu	a title usually indicating respect
bela	a sweet-smelling white flower, similar to jasmine
besan	flour made from grams
Bhai	brother
Bhasmasura	a devil in Hindu mythology, given the power, by God Shiva, to turn to ashes anybody on whose head he placed his hand
bindi	a dot, usually made with red powder, worn on the forehead by Hindu women
bidi	inexpensive country cigarette made of tobacco rolled in a leaf.
Bua	father's sister in Hindu families
burqa	a robe with a veil worn by Muslim ladies
Chacha	father's brother
Chachi	father's brother's wife
chapati	thin, flat unleavened bread, usually prepared from wheat
Dada	paternal grandfather
Dadi	paternal grandmother
dal	pulses or lentils, usally cooked like a soup or sauce, to be eaten with rice and chapatis
Deepavali	Hindu festival of lights, marking the beginning of the Hindu year and celebrating the victory of light over darkness
doma	a person belonging to the lowest caste, associated with burning of dead bodies
dupatta	long thin scarf worn over the shoulders and sometimes over the head by women in North India

gharara	loose, ankle-length divided skirt worn by Muslim ladies
hai dit Rama	a prayer beseeching God Rama's benevolence
halwa	a sweet dish or pudding
Id	Muslim festival at the end of Ramzan, the month of fasting
jelabi	a sweet made of flour, fried in oil and filled with syrup
Janab	an honorific prefix attached to the name of Muslim men
jawan	a soldier
ji	an honorific suffix attached to Indian names or titles
kattha	catechu; astringent substance with tannin from bark used in betel
kewra	a sweet-smelling flower
Khala	mother's sister in Muslim families
kheer	a sweet dish prepared from rice, milk and sugar
kurta	a loose shirt without collar and cuffs
laddu	a round sweet
Lakshmi	Hindu goddess of wealth
lungi	a length of cloth, about two-and-a-half metres, usually worn by Muslim men, tied round the waist and reaching the ankles
Marwari	a prominent business sub-caste in India
mehtar	a low-caste person who is a scavenger by occupation
Miyan	a respectful suffix added to the name of Muslim men
paan	betel leaf, chewing of which is common in India, and which contains lime and betel nut
Pashmina	a special kind of wool made from the hair of the Pashmina goat, found in Kashmir
puri	unleavened fried bread
Ram nam sat hai! Sabki yahi gat hai!	literally, 'Rama's name is the truth! This is everybody's fate!' A refrain chanted when a corpse is carried to the cremation site
sahib	a respectful suffix added on to the names of men
sardar	literally 'chief'; respectful form of address for a Sikh man

sari	a length of cloth, usually about six metres, worn by Indian women
seth	a rich businessman
sheesham	a kind of tree
tazia	model of the tomb of Imam Husain carried in procession on the occasion of Muhurrum
Teeja	a festival held on the third day of the lunar fortnight, in the month of Savan
tulsi	an aromatic shrub holding a religious significance for Hindus
Vaid	a medical practitioner of the ayurvedic medical system
veer	a brave soldier
zakat	a kind of tax incumbent on Muslims in which they have to give one-fortieth of their annual income to charity

BIOGRAPHICAL NOTES

Amarkant
Born in 1925 in Ballia District, UP, he was educated at Ballia and Allahabad. His published works include several collections of short stories and novels. He received the Soviet Land Nehru Award for his novel, *Sookha Patta*. Amarkant worked in the editorial department of a daily newspaper in Agra and is currently associated with the magazine, *Manorama*, published from Allahabad.

Abdul Bismillah
Born in 1949 in Allahabad District, UP, Bismillah studied Hindi literature at Allahabad University. He has published three novels, four collections of short stories and three collections of poems. He received the 1987 Soviet Land Nehru Award for his novel, *Jhini Jhini Bini Chadariya*. At present he teaches Hindi at the Jamia Millia Islamia University, New Delhi.

Vijay Chauhan
Born in 1931 in Jabalpur, MP, Vijay Chauhan was educated at Jabalpur and Delhi. A collection of his short stories, *Mizraab*, was published in 1972, and another, *Ekantvas*, posthumously in 1989. Vijay Chauhan taught at Saugor, where he was associated with a theatre group called Prayog. He lived in the USA from the 1970s till his death in 1988.

Gajanan Madhav Muktibodh
Born in 1917 in Sheopur, Gwalior, Muktibodh studied at Nagpur University. He started teaching at the Barnagar Middle School in 1937. Thereafter, he undertook various teaching and journalistic assignments in Ujjain, Varanasi, Calcutta, Bombay, Bangalore and Jabalpur. He is well-known and highly respected as a poet, short story writer and essayist. Muktibodh died in 1964 after a protracted illness.

Kunwar Narayan

Born in 1927 in Faizabad, UP, he studied English literature at Lucknow University. His publications include various collections of poems and one of short stories. In 1971 Narayan received an award from the Hindustani Academy for his long poem, *Atmajayi*. He has done editorial work with *Yugchetna* for five years and has travelled in Eastern Europe and China. At present he lives in Lucknow.

Mehrunnisa Parvez

Born in 1944 in Balaghat District, MP, she is a freelance writer. Her first story appeared in *Dharmayug* in 1963. Thereafter, she has been widely published in various Hindi magazines. She has written fourteen literary books and several articles on social problems. She is associated with various organizations working to foster communal harmony. At present she lives in Bhopal.

Uday Prakash

Born in 1952 near Chhatisgarh, MP, he studied at Jawaharlal Nehru University, New Delhi. After a brief teaching assignment and a short tenure with the Times Research Institute of Social Science, he did some editorial work with *Dinmaan* and *Sunday*. His published works include a volume of verse and a collection of short stories. Uday Prakash was awarded the Bharat Bhushan Agarwal Award for his poem, *Tibet*, and the Om Prakash Award for his collection of short stories, *Daryai Ghora*. At present he lives in Delhi.

Usha Priyamvada

She studied English literature at Allahabad University which she later taught at the same university. She also taught for several years at Lady Shri Ram College, New Delhi. Her publications include three collections of short stories and two novels. She has also translated *Mirabai* into English. Usha Priyamvada has lived in the USA for several years and teaches at the University of Wisconsin.

Zahra Rai

Born in 1922 in Varanasi, UP, Zahra Rai studied at Vasant College, Varanasi and the Benaras Hindu University. She started writing in the 1950s and her first story, written under a pseudonym, appeared in *Kahani* in 1955. Since then she has published many short stories in Hindi and Urdu. She has contributed various feature articles on gardening and music to Hindi and English language magazines. She has been an exponent of Indian classical vocal music, which she also taught for some time. At present she is the principal of a school in Allahabad.

Mohan Rakesh

Born in 1925 in Amritsar, Rakesh was educated at Hindu College, Amritsar, and Oriental College, Lahore. After teaching at Elphinstone College, Bombay, and D.A.V. College, Jalandhar, he resigned to adopt writing as an independent vocation. He edited the *Sarika* for a year in Bombay and was one of the pioneers of the New Story. He has published six collections of short stories, two novels, three plays and some translations. He was the recipient of the Sangeet Natak Akademi Award, the President's Gold Medal, the Padmashree, which he refused, and the Nehru Fellowship for research on *The Dramatic Word*. He died in 1972.

Ramkumar

Born in 1924 in Shimla, his publications include novels, short stories and a travelogue. A collection of his short stories has appeared in English translation published by the Writers' Workshop, Calcutta. One of India's foremost painters, Ramkumar has spent two years in Paris studying art and has held exhibitions in India, Europe and America. In 1970 he spent eight months in USA on a Rockefeller Foundation grant. At present he lives in New Delhi.

Sanjeev

Born in 1947 in Sultanpur District, UP, Sanjeev was educated in West Bengal. Known for his committed writing, he has published four collections of short stories, four novels, a children's novel and a play. At present he is Senior Chemist in the Central Growth Works, Kulti, West Bengal.

Ramnarayan Shukla

Born in 1937 in Fatehpur District, UP, Ramnarayan Shukla passed his B.Com. from Calcutta University and commenced studying Law, a course that he left unfinished. From 1962 till 1967, he did editorial work with *Kahani* and *Yuvak Darpan*. He died of meningitis at Delhi in 1968. His short stories, most of which were published in various magazines during his lifetime, have been compiled in three volumes.

Nirmal Verma

Born in 1929 in Shimla, he studied history at St. Stephen's College, Delhi, and has taught for a number of years. One of the leading figures in the New Story movement, Nirmal Verma has published several collections of short stories, essays, travelogues and novels, including *Ek Chithra Sukh* and his most recent *Raat Ka Reporter*. After working for a well-known English daily newspaper, he lived in Czechoslovakia for several years where he studied and translated Czech literature. He has travelled extensively in Europe and at present lives in New Delhi, writing fiction.

Shrikant Verma

Born in 1931 in Bilaspur, MP, Shrikant Verma studied Hindi literature at Nagpur University and is well-known for his poetry, short stories, novels and criticism. He has also translated Pasternak, Lorca and Wallace Stevens. He did editorial work with various Hindi periodicals, including *Dinmaan*, and was twice elected a Member of Parliament from M.P. in 1976 and 1982. He received several awards including the Sahitya Kala Parishad Award in 1982 and the Sahitya Academy Award posthumously in 1987. He travelled extensively in Europe, China, Japan and Canada. He was poet-in-residence in the International Writing Programme of the University of Iowa in 1970 and 1978. He died in 1986.